RAINBOW FILTH

TIM MEYER

Ghoulish Books
an imprint of Perpetual Motion Machine Publishing
San Antonio, Texas

Rainbow Filth
Copyright © 2023 Tim Meyer

www.GhoulishBooks.com

Cover by Matthew Revert

This one's for the *Goosebumps* kids out there, like me.
Keep it cool, keep it weird.

Recording

Property of the
Shrewsbury Police

Saturday/June 2nd, 2024/5:48 p.m.
Interviewing Detective: Chase MacDonald
Witness/Suspect: Adam Godfrey

DETECTIVE MACDONALD: More coffee, Adam?

ADAM: No, thank you.

DETECTIVE MACDONALD: Cigarette?

ADAM: Don't smoke.

DETECTIVE MACDONALD: Really? *[shuffling of paperwork]* My mistake. I assumed, you know, since you were into heavy drugs and all, that you might be a smoker.

ADAM: That's quite an assumption, Detective.

DETECTIVE MACDONALD: Like I said, my mistake. Do you mind if we get down to it? The reason you're here?

ADAM: I prefer it, actually.

DETECTIVE MACDONALD: Perfect. Can you go back to that night, the night of your professor's *disappearance*, and tell me how it was you came to congregate?

TIM MEYER

[silence]

DETECTIVE MACDONALD: Sorry, did I say something to offend you?

ADAM: No, just . . .

DETECTIVE MACDONALD: What? What is it?

[silence]

DETECTIVE MACDONALD: We don't have all night, Adam. Don't know about you, but I'd love to go home. See the wife and kiss the kids goodnight. The only thing holding that up is you and *your* story, which, I might add, isn't making a lick of sense, so I'd really appreciate it if you'd stop clenching that asshole of yours and just speak, preferably the truth. That's all I'm interested in, Adam—the truth. Nothing more, nothing less.

ADAM: Already said everything there is to say.

DETECTIVE MACDONALD: Well, your professor is still missing and we have . . . well, no leads on the other . . . what should I call them? *Students* doesn't seem like the correct word in this situation.

ADAM: *Students* is accurate.

DETECTIVE MACDONALD: I prefer the term "test subjects." Would that be more accurate than students?

[silence]

DETECTIVE MACDONALD: See, from my understanding, a student is someone who learns. For the life of me, I can't figure out what that professor of yours was teaching.

ADAM: He was teaching us magic.

DETECTIVE MACDONALD: [scoffing] Teaching you magic? Well, you have a wild imagination, that's for sure. You mind telling me the story again? Please, Adam. I'm begging you. And start with the truth this time.

ADAM: Are you sure?

DETECTIVE MACDONALD: Am I sure about what?

ADAM: . . . That you want the truth?

DETECTIVE MACDONALD: Look at this badge, asshole. [something hitting the table] This badge stands for the truth. I stand for the truth. The truth is all I'm after.

ADAM: Okay. But will you believe me?

DETECTIVE MACDONALD: That depends.

ADAM: On what?

DETECTIVE MACDONALD: On how convincing you are.

ADAM: I'll tell you the truth. Under one condition.

DETECTIVE MACDONALD: You ain't exactly in a position to make demands, but I'm entertaining all offers.

ADAM: You let me go. You believe me and let me go.

DETECTIVE MACDONALD: I can't promise that.

ADAM: I didn't do anything wrong.

DETECTIVE MACDONALD: I beg to differ. Experimenting with the stuff you were experimenting with ain't exactly legal.

ADAM: But no one knows about it yet. How can that be illegal?

DETECTIVE MACDONALD: Listen to me. Your professor was into some shady shit, okay? You let us worry about that. Let me hear the story, and then I'll decide how innocent you are. Okay? Sound good?

[silence]

ADAM: Okay. I'll tell the story.

DETECTIVE MACDONALD: Thank Christ.

ADAM: Just try not to scream.

DETECTIVE MACDONALD: [humorless laugh] Okay, pal. You just worry about being truthful.

ADAM: The truth. Yeah, sure—I can do that. But you won't believe it. No one will.

I met Professor Lewis Hauser during my first semester at Bordentown State College. He was giving a lecture about unusual pharmaceutical applications to treat anxiety, and, not being a psychology major, I couldn't give less of a shit about the lecture itself—I was there for another reason.

Lizzette Carrillo.

Liz was the perfect girl. Cute, smart, funny (hilarious actually), and even though she was way out of my league (several leagues out), she liked me. It was one of those "just friends" relationships that matured over our freshman year. I met her in the cafeteria of all places, and in one of those cliché high school cute-meet scenarios, I knocked into her and spilled a bottle of natural green tea all over her UGGs. It was a disaster, and I thought I was going to die right there, but she'd been cool about it. I helped her clean up the mess to the best of our capabilities and then we proceeded to talk, and she was easy to talk to. Man, we just had the coolest, most natural conversation in the world. I can't even remember everything we chatted about, small talk really, but it was a solid twenty minutes of back-and-forth with no awkward pauses. Not to mention, there wasn't a moment of hostility on her end regarding the spill. She was gracious, didn't yell at me for ruining her boots (I assumed they were ruined but possibly not), or call me stupid, clumsy, or a fool—insults I deserved. She was just cool, man. Cool as whip.

But you want me to focus on Professor Hauser, though. Right? That's what you want to hear? Not about Liz, even though Liz is a part of this—a *huge* part of this—and what came later.

Anyway, I went to see Hauser's lecture because of her, because we weren't officially dating at the time—stuck in that awful phase between being exclusive but not putting labels on the relationship, more high school shit that carried over to the college years—and I wanted to be super close to her, be around her every damn second I could. So, Hauser's speech was on a Tuesday night, and we went, and I couldn't concentrate on the lecture itself because I was too nervous about deciding whether I should hold her hand or keep public physical contact to a minimum, if any at all. I opted to keep my hands in my pockets and play it cool.

Cool as whip.

Hauser spoke of pharmaceutical treatments in extreme cases of anxiety, and he got really animated during a twenty-minute tangent about psychedelics and the positive contributions they have to the medical field. Most of the rant went in one ear and out the other, but I couldn't ignore the man's passion for the subject. I got the sense that he'd prefer to discuss these particular drugs and their effects on open minds over what the lecture was initially about. At one point, I felt like I was listening to some old hippy talk about the seventies and how great it was to trip out on the drugs of the time. Like reading Hunter S. Thompson's *Fear and Loathing in Las Vegas* but without the political and social commentary. Just the trippy parts. Which—let's be honest—are the best parts.

Whatever. I'm rambling again. Arrest me.

(that's a joke, Detective, calm down)

Let me just finish this introduction by saying Hauser was built for the part of the psychedelic enthusiast. He was young compared to the university's other faculty members that I'd interacted with, mid-forties, but looked like any face you'd find at a Janis Joplin concert back in the day. He had a beard that was probably deemed unruly by professional standards, John Lennon reading glasses he wore one-hundred percent of the time, and a shaggy head of curly hair that fell in around the ears. I never saw him without his tan tweed jacket, complete with elbow patches, which was fraying near the cuffs.

Hauser was the kind of guy you immediately wanted to like, even though I didn't. And that was only because of the way he looked at my girl.

I kissed Liz in the parking lot later that evening after the lecture concluded. I remember the kiss specifically because it was one of the first times she introduced a little tongue to the party. We'd been pretty new as an "unofficial" couple at that point, and we hadn't even seen each other completely naked yet. There was no sex during the first couple of weeks of dating. She wasn't like that. Not that she wanted to wait until marriage or anything, but she wanted to be in a stable relationship before ticking that box. I understood. To be honest, I kinda liked that about her. It was different from most of the other girls I'd met that freshman year. Most of them only wanted to fool around and weren't looking for anything serious—which I was totally okay with too. Absolutely nothing wrong with the occasional dorm room fling. But Liz—man, things were just different between us. Emotional fireworks popped off every time we stepped in the same room together. She didn't tell me, but I could tell she felt it too.

Anyway, we were smooching in the parking lot, and Hauser approached us. At first he looked like he'd come to break up the party, but then he just looked at us and smiled like, *Oh, aren't you two cute?* It was kind of weird the way he looked at us, and I'm not gonna lie—I got some pervy vibes from him. But then again, I'd only known the guy two seconds. And maybe he knew Liz better than I originally thought, which would explain why he even approached us mid-smooch in the first place.

Turned out, he did know her pretty well.

"Hey, Liz," he said, and I immediately disliked the guy the second he opened his mouth. Fair or not—that's the truth. "Thank you so much for stopping by tonight."

"Oh," she said, pulling off me and wiping my saliva from her lips with the back of her hand. "Hey, Professor Hauser."

"Please," he said, grinning foolishly. "I've told you a thousand times, you can call me Lewis. Actually, I prefer *Lew*."

"*Lew*." She giggled, and envy flowered within me. She never giggled that way when I told a dumb joke or said something mildly humorous, yet speaking his nickname alone was enough to elicit that reaction. "I thought the lecture was very informative. I look forward to more."

"Well, you should sign up for my Advanced Therapeutic Applications course next semester. Doing a whole section on psychedelics and the benefits of experimental pharmacology."

"Sounds amazing."

Sounded fucking dangerous to me, but who the fuck was I to argue? I was too busy studying *Lew's* intent. I wasn't sure if he was playing the role of an overachieving college professor or if he was trying to bang my future girlfriend. And since I couldn't rightfully tell, the jealous male in me went with the latter.

"Who's the boyfriend?" he asked, switching his gaze to me. "Hi there—Lewis Hauser. You can call me Lewis or Lew. Doesn't matter."

I shook his hand even though it felt like I was betraying myself. "Name's Adam. Adam Godfrey."

"Godfrey." He shook my hand quite vigorously, like I was the president or something. Someone with tremendous prestige. Couldn't tell if he was lowkey mocking me or not. In the end I can only assume he wasn't. That was just his way. Always overacting everything. Would have been a hell of a drama professor. "Meaning God or good, -frey coming from the Germanic term 'frid', meaning *peace*."

"That's right," I replied, like I knew this all long. Like, of course I researched my own surname to know what it meant. *Of course.* "You sure know your stuff."

He winked as if to say, *You're damn right I do*.

Then he took back his hand. I wanted to grip it, hold on, flaunt a little tough-guy elbow grease, but I wasn't that guy. "Liz is a great girl," he said, like I didn't already know it. "You're a lucky dude."

I only eyed him.

"You two have a great night. Liz, I'll see you tomorrow."

She said her goodbye. I watched the bastard walk to his forty-year-old station wagon that had the entire back covered with bumper stickers. I wasn't close enough to read any of them, but they looked like the political and social variety. A few band logos. I think I saw a bong on one of them, which I was like—why the hell would you put a police target on your back, you stupid idiot? Also interesting that he parked that piece in the same lot as the other professors.

I watched Hauser drive away. He pressed two fingers to his lips as if blowing us a kiss and then gave us a wave.

Us.

No, that kiss/wave was meant for Liz and Liz alone.

I was sure of it.

Over the next few months, Liz and I became "official." I know—I sound like a stupid high school kid with a puppy-love crush, but let's be honest; I was only a year out of high school and finding my way through this new adventure life had thrown my way, and I was really excited to finally be introduced as Liz's new "boyfriend."

New.

Meaning, there were those who came before me.

Meaning, there were other guys she'd fucked before me.

I don't know why but I was immediately jealous of them too. Didn't know their names, didn't know what they looked like, but I couldn't help but want to track down each one of them and knock on their doors, introduce myself, and let them know I was now sleeping with their ex.

Petty.

Stupid.

I was being a pathetic boy-child, sure. But as quickly as those jackassy thoughts passed through my head, they left, and I decided then I'd be mature about the whole thing—be sure to remind myself that I was no longer in high school, and that sort of behavior was of someone who hadn't grown up yet.

And I had grown up.

I was never the biggest kid during my elementary and middle school days. In high school, I was always the skinniest, smallest kid in class, which made my body prime real estate for the bullies to invest in. For some reason—I dunno, maybe because I was *too* easy of a target—I didn't get bullied the worst. The worst one to get it in my graduating class was a kid named Jordan Diel. Poor kid was once stuffed in a gym locker for three hours. When they finally got him out, he was hospitalized and put on oxygen. Spent the whole day hooked up to a tank.

Anyway, not to diverge from the main point of all this, but the fact was—some kids had it worse. I was lucky.

So why act this way? Now?

I don't know other than I was in love with Liz Carrillo, and love makes you do some crazy stupid shit sometimes. Makes you think differently. Did you know that love can change the chemical properties that make up your brain, akin to being high? Did you know that shit? Crazy stuff, neuropeptides. Look it up if you get a chance. The mind is fascinating.

Anyway, getting back on track—our relationship evolved over freshman year and beyond. I met Liz's parents, and she met mine. We drove to the shore and spent entire days walking the boardwalks, holding each other's hands. We got out of New Jersey as much as our full-time class schedules and part-time work schedules would allow. Weekend getaways to New York City and Connecticut. Maine in the summers, renting log cabins in the woods two weeks at a time just to escape society. No cell phones, no connections to social media; just us and the cabin and the mountains and the state parks that seemed almost endless by design.

It was junior year, during one of those Maine excursions, that Liz surprised me.

"Want to try mushrooms?" she asked one night. She unzipped a designer pouch smaller than her wallet and extracted a clear baggy. Inside were pieces of what I assumed were the aforementioned mushrooms.

"Mushrooms?" I'd never experimented with anything other than pot before. I smoked occasionally throughout high school and college, and never considered myself a major stoner or anything like that. I'd only done cocaine once in my life, at a high school party, and I hated it, detested everything about the experience. It kinda made me swear off all other drugs. So, when faced with the opportunity to ingest some mind-altering substance from a girl with whom I had fallen deeply in love . . . it wasn't an easy choice. "I've never done mushrooms."

"I know," she said, smiling. "You told me."

We'd smoked together over the years, and I was sure the subject had come up, but I don't remember ever divulging how I truly felt about the harder stuff or my inexperience with them. Her marijuana use could be considered casual too—a few times a month if that. At parties and small social gatherings. As I understood it, she never smoked alone.

But Liz's offering made me suspect she was dabbling in certain substances without my knowledge.

"I guess?" I didn't want to sound *uncool* to my girlfriend of two and a half years. Even though I know she wouldn't think differently of me. But, at the same time, it felt like a test. Like, if I said "no," then what? Would I be good enough to date? Would she end things? Probably not, but when you love someone that much, you don't want to give them any reason to let you go. "Sure—fuck it. We're on vacation, right?"

"That's the spirit," she said, shaking the mushrooms out onto a paper plate. They looked like mushrooms enough. Dome-shaped heads and tails as long as my finger. The juvenile part of my brain thought they looked like skinny penises.

She went over to the kitchenette and made two cups of tea. After bringing them back over to the couch, she handed me one, then soaked a single mushroom in her drink. She did the same for the cup she handed me. We waited about five minutes. "Ready?"

"Ready as I'll ever be."

She took the first sip. Then invited me to do the same.

"Clear your head, though. If you're harboring negative thoughts, you might have a bad trip."

I was with her; there were no negative thoughts.

We drank the tea, giggled, and although I didn't have the hallucinogenic experienced that I'd always heard about—though I did stop and just stare out the window for about twenty minutes straight—I did have a pretty good time.

Recording
Property of the Shrewsbury Police

Saturday/June 2nd, 2024/6:32 p.m.
Interviewing Detective: Chase MacDonald
Witness: Adam Godfrey

DETECTIVE MACDONALD: Why the fuck are you telling me all of this?

ADAM: You asked.

DETECTIVE MACDONALD: I asked about Hauser. I asked about *that* night. You know what I want to know, I don't know why you're telling me all this . . . this stuff. I'm not interested in your fucking love life, kid.

ADAM: In order to understand the thing that took place that night, you have to understand me. Liz. Hauser. The others. You have to understand the past to understand—

DETECTIVE MACDONALD: Cut the shit. I'm not interested in your hippy psychobabble. I've already got you admitting to me that you're a huge druggie, so I don't know how well this will go for you. Jesus, man. Why would you even admit that stuff to me? You realize you're speaking to a detective, right?

ADAM: What are you going to do? Arrest me? (*cuffs rattle*)

DETECTIVE MACDONALD: Touché.

ADAM: Anyway. You asked for the story, I'm going to give you the whole story. I want you to understand everything. Maybe it will help.

DETECTIVE MACDONALD: I don't think there's any helping you. We found you at the scene of the crime, blood all over your clothes. Hauser's blood.

ADAM: Allegedly.

DETECTIVE MACDONALD: What do you think we are? Fucking amateurs? Initial labs came back earlier today. Hauser's blood checks out. We just need the body. Or, more accurately, where you put the body.

ADAM: And the other blood on my clothes? Who did that belong to?

(*Silence*)

DETECTIVE MACDONALD: Still checking that out. We'll get there. When the full labs come back, we'll let you know. Unless you want to volunteer the information. Sure you still don't want a lawyer, kid?

ADAM: I don't need a lawyer.

DETECTIVE MACDONALD: No?

ADAM: I'm innocent.

DETECTIVE MACDONALD: Sure you are, pal.

ADAM: I'll finish my story. And then we'll see.

DETECTIVE MACDONALD: I'm all ears.

We didn't experiment with drugs again until later that year, the following semester. The second time I met Professor Lewis Hauser. Lewis. *Lew*.

Asshole.

I'd almost forgot the man existed until I met him again. Then the memories of that night came back, his lecture almost three years ago. He looked the same as he had. Hadn't aged a day since that night. I was surprised that Liz kept in contact with him. I mean, was it normal to engage in a friendly relationship with your professor throughout the entirety of your collegiate career? I guess it happened, but I never spoke with any of my college professors after our classes ended, not even via email. But Lewis—he was different, all right. I could tell from that first night that he was the kind of educator who wanted to be friends with all his students, who wanted to fit in with them, blurring that line of professionalism in a way that I—personally—found kinda icky.

Oh, he was also the kind of professor that came off like he wanted to sleep with them, too. You know the type. Or maybe you don't—but I'm sure you can use your imagination, Detective.

He was suave. I'll give him that.

We met in an empty lecture hall in the Farrow building, on the far west end of campus. It backed up to the mountains that overlooked all of Bordentown State. A secluded building, one few had the purpose of visiting unless there was a lecture taking place. Tonight, the building belonged to Hauser and his loyal following of scholars. There were six of us. Me, Liz. Billy Leak and

Deana Morris. They were a couple that Liz and I went out with quite often, double dates to dinner and the movies every other weekend when we weren't cramming for tests or catching up on sleep. The other two that made up Hauser's cult were the Hurt brothers, Russell and Arthur. Twins. Identical. It was difficult telling the two apart, but one had a broken nose that never healed right, via a flying elbow in a high school soccer match. He joked about it, said he liked the whole "Owen Wilson" thing he had going on, but seriously? He didn't look like Owen Wilson or have his distinctive nose. The bone was only slightly off and you had to get real close to notice it. It took me meeting him three times to remember that it was Russell with the busted schnozz. Good guys—the kind of friends who seemed like they'd go out of their way to do anything for you, like bring you food when you're sick or pick you up when your car breaks down—but also, they were crazy stoners who were high more often than not. They were also hilarious and generally entertaining, fun to be around. That is, if they liked you. If you were in their crew.

Hauser welcomed us, shook our hands, and then we proceeded to eat brownies (sans weed) and enjoy some beer that Billy had brought. He worked at a local brewery when he wasn't studying to become a chemist, so he always had some cool new local brew to try, something that tasted a far cry away from the watered-down, filtered lagers we could typically afford on our student budget, the kind you could get on special for less than fifty cents a can. He typically brought heavy stuff I couldn't drink more than one or two of—double IPAs and chocolate stouts that neared the 11% ABV range.

Deana and Liz were best friends. Had been since high school. Deana wanted to go to Bordentown ever since her freshman year of high school (a family tradition) and it was Liz who followed her here because the two were practically inseparable. Sometimes Liz chose hanging out with Deana over me, and that was cool I guess because Deana had been there first, but at the same time I was always kinda resentful because it seemed like it was never the other way around. Deana always chose Billy when the situation was reversed. If Liz needed her best friend and Deana had plans with Billy, the plans with Billy always won out. But if Deana needed Liz for something, needed a girl's night out or a *Real Housewives* marathon, then whatever we had on the agenda was immediately tossed aside and the girls would go do their thing. It wasn't fair, but oh well—that's the way life goes sometimes.

My personal opinion, of course, but Deana wasn't a very good best friend.

Hauser started that evening like any other, so I'm told. He recited a joke. Some dad joke, a really lame one. Can't remember exactly what it was other than it caused me to roll my eyes so hard my retinas ached for the next three hours. Then he turned to me and made me introduce myself, told me to give the small group one fact about myself. Could be anything.

"My name is Adam Godfrey," I said, laughing because the whole thing was stupid. This wasn't a class. I wasn't obligated to be there. I was only there for Liz. If I knew then what I know now, I would have told Hauser to fuck his own mouth and then punched out his teeth to make it easier for him to do so. "One fact about me . . . let me see. Well, there's nothing really that interesting about me."

"Oh, come on," Hauser said, and now it was his turn to roll his eyes. "There's gotta be *something* interesting about you, Godfrey. Otherwise, Liz wouldn't have even bothered with your lame ass."

The Liz comment felt like an aggressive jab, but everyone laughed, so I chalked it up to me being overdefensive in these types of social situations.

"Yeah, I guess that's true," I admitted. I said to Liz, "Want to help me out, love?"

Before she could even consider it, Hauser clicked his tongue twice. "No, no. This is a one-man show. The stage is yours and yours alone. Come on—tell us. One interesting fact. One thing that no one else knows about you. Not even Liz."

Now I had to dig deep. There wasn't too much Liz didn't know about me. "Oh God. Okay. This one time at band camp . . . "

Everyone waited for me to finish. No one got the reference. If they did, no one rolled their eyes or acknowledged it. It was totally lame.

"Okay, never mind then. Fuck—okay. Um, I stole a hundred dollars once."

"Really?" Liz said, crossing her arms. "Like, recently?"

"No," I said, laughing through my nose. "No, this was in high school. Sophomore year. I was working at a hardware store in my hometown. I don't even know why I did it. I didn't necessarily even need the money. Wasn't desperate or anything. I just took it because I . . . because I could, I guess? Maybe I just needed to know *if* I could do it. Like, some sort of challenge."

"You criminal," Hauser said, deadpan. No smirk. His eyes bored into me, and I felt their heat on my cheeks.

"What?" I said, trying to keep the situation light. When I'd walked in there, I thought this was a friendly, judgment-free zone, and I could have admitted anything—well, almost anything—in that moment and no one would have thought of me any different. But now . . . now I wasn't so sure. "It was years ago. I was practically a kid. We all do dumb stuff when—"

"You stole a hundred dollars," Hauser said, moving around me in a circle, like a shark sizing up its prey. "From a mom-and-pop hardware store? That's taking food out of someone's mouth, Godfrey."

"Look, man. I didn't—"

Hauser waved off any excuse I was about to come up with. "How could you? How *dare* you."

I saw Liz tighten up, her body wriggle as if the bones beneath her flesh were infested with worms. Like she wanted to shrink into a ball and roll away.

"Man, it was just a stupid mistake," I said. "What's—"

I shut my mouth and watched a wide jester's grin spill across Hauser's face.

"Ahhhhhh," he said, pointing at me, his other hand over his chest as he arched back, laughing toward the ceiling. "Gotcha, Godfrey."

The rest of the room laughed along with him. The band around my chest finally snapped and I could breathe again.

"You had me for a second," I said.

Liz came up and put her arms around my waist, stood on her toes and pecked my cheek. "My little thief," she said.

All felt miraculously right in the world.

Later, Hauser broke out a bottle of pills. One for each of us. The pills were teal-colored, about the size of a baby aspirin. Hardly anything that looked menacing, though a bottle of unlabeled pharmaceuticals was, I guess, enough to put me on the fence. Especially since I wasn't sold on the cut of Hauser's jib. But Liz trusted him enough to pop that sucker in her mouth the second it graced her palm. She handed me one and smiled.

"It's safe," she said, reading my face. "Just a low-grade muscle relaxer. Will smooth you out, especially mixed with the alcohol."

"Best sleep you'll ever get tonight," Hauser assured me.

"You'll wake up like a totally new person," Billy added, punching me lightly on the arm.

The twins giggled as they popped their pills, swallowed them with a swig of IPA.

I took the pill and hesitated. More so because—even though Liz was free to do as she pleased—it felt like she had this whole secret life that I never knew about. This whole 'drug culture' thing. I don't mean to sound too judgy, but it became this unexpected element of our relationship, and I didn't know how to feel about it. Like, there was this whole other part of her I wasn't privy to in the last three years. I mean, we spent a lot of time together. We were together more often than not. But there were times when she was off doing her own thing, and I started to wonder if that thing included getting high and tripping out on experimental psychedelics with this asshole professor and the small drug cult he was accumulating.

I wasn't overbearing. I wasn't the boyfriend who needed to know where their significant other was all the time. I wasn't that guy at all. I trusted Liz. Beyond anything. She could have told me the most insane lie, and I would have believed it. So . . . this was sending off all types of red flags. But those flags were easily ignored because, again, in the end, I did not want to fight with her, give her any reason to flee, break up with me, end things.

I kicked back the pill and swallowed it dry.

Twenty minutes later, I felt it. It did even me out, and I felt almost numb. Not just my body and limbs, but my mind too. I didn't even ask what the name of the pill was—didn't really care.

It was around then that Hauser began talking about drugs and pharmacology and various experimental psychedelics he'd taken over the years. I tuned most of it out and only came back to the conversation when he started discussing an upcoming trip. I didn't know if he meant *trip* as a *hallucinatory experience* or if he was taking a vacation somewhere, but once I got my feet on the ground and focused, I understood he was going on an actual excursion to a secluded jungle in Cambodia.

"Deep jungle," he said. "We have a guide and everything."

I shook my head, not understanding. "We?"

Liz licked her lips. Dodged my gaze.

"Wait," Hauser said, running his hand through his mane of hair. "You didn't tell him?"

"Tell me what?" I watched the other eyes in the room settle on something else. The twins pretended to hold a private conversation, turning their backs to us.

"I meant to," Liz said, her voice small, "but it just never came up."

"Oh," Hauser said, twirling, doing a full three-sixty, smiling, and then covering that smile with both hands. "Oh, this is rich."

Liz turned to me. "Babe. I've been meaning to tell you. I'm going on a little vacation with the group."

I couldn't believe what I was hearing. I wasn't mad at the trip—she could go anywhere she liked, didn't matter to me—I was mad she didn't tell me. "Oh. How long?" I tried to keep from turning red, but I felt the burn on my cheeks begin to spread.

"Two weeks," Hauser said.

"Two weeks?" I asked Liz, pretending Hauser didn't exist. "You'll be gone for two weeks and you didn't tell me?"

"I meant to, I'm sorry."

I wanted to get mad but couldn't. I wanted to turn around and punch Hauser in the face but couldn't. There were a thousand things I wanted to scream and shout but couldn't. In the end, I said, "Okay."

"Okay? Like . . . you're not mad?"

"I mean, I wish you had told me. But no . . . not mad."

She threw her arms around me and squeezed my neck. Kissed my cheek. Then my lips. I hoped it made Hauser sick, made him want to puke.

"Thank you." Her eyes were almost luminous. "I'll make it up to you."

She kissed me again, confirmation that all was right with the world.

Recording

Property of the Shrewsbury Police

Saturday/June 2nd, 2024/6:58 p.m.
Interviewing Detective: Chase MacDonald
Witness/Suspect: Adam Godfrey

DETECTIVE MACDONALD: So you just let your girlfriend go off to Cambodia with some druggie adjunct professor? (*scoffs*) Wow. You really are a spineless little piece of shit, huh?

ADAM: What was I going to do? *Not* let her go?

DETECTIVE MACDONALD: That's what I would have done. If I really cared about her. You know how dangerous this trip could have been? Hiking in the jungle with a bunch of amateurs and one crazy-ass professor who—you have to admit—at this point in the story, you were made well aware he wasn't playing with a full deck of cards.

ADAM: I'll admit that, yes. I knew Hauser was . . . eccentric. Possibly dangerous. I mean, the guy was handing out drugs to his students for shit's sake. And I hated that I wasn't invited. On the trip, I mean. I felt like I was intentionally left out. I trusted Liz, but I didn't trust Hauser. Not a smidge.

DETECTIVE MACDONALD: Why were you left out?

ADAM: Wasn't part of the crew yet, I guess. Liz told me later that Hauser had major trust issues, and the trip didn't exactly hold any scholarly merit, at least in the university's eyes, should they ever know about it. She made it seem like it was a risk that *I* even knew about it, but Liz told him the only way she could go was *if* I knew about it. She couldn't disappear for two weeks without me losing my mind and alerting the authorities. So, she had to tell me. I guess, now that I look back on it, it was a symbol of our love.

DETECTIVE MACDONALD: *(scoffs)* How so?

ADAM: She could have broken it off with me then disappeared for two weeks. I wouldn't have asked any questions then.

DETECTIVE MACDONALD: True. Symbol of love might be pushing it, but . . . the girl loves you. Congratulations. Very happy for you. Wanna skip to the part where this all starts to make some fucking sense to me? What does a trip to Cambodia have to do with what happened the day your friends ghosted off the face of the universe?

ADAM: It has everything to do with what happened that day.

DETECTIVE MACDONALD: Explain. Double time.

ADAM: They went there for a specific experience.

DETECTIVE MACDONALD: You're being vague. I don't like it.

ADAM: Let's just say, it isn't easy to explain.

DETECTIVE MACDONALD: Just say they went there to get high.

ADAM: It's more than that, though.

DETECTIVE MACDONALD: How so?

ADAM: They went there to discover a very specific psychedelic property exclusive to that particular region of the world. It's so rare and powerful that few people on the planet know where it's located. Apparently, Hauser had some connections, and the group headed to Cambodia to look for it.

DETECTIVE MACDONALD: This drug have a name?

ADAM: Nope. Nothing official. But we came to know it as *The Rainbow Filth*.

DETECTIVE MACDONALD: (*snorting*) Sounds like a terrible hair-metal band from the 80s. Or a Dio album.

ADAM: It might be both. But it was an appropriate name for the stuff.

DETECTIVE MACDONALD: What was the source? Did it come from a plant? A wild mushroom? I mean, gotta be honest—I'm no expert on advanced psychedelics, so you'll have to help me out.

ADAM: I'm no expert either. Hauser's the one you'll want to talk to for specifics, but he's . . . uh . . . not exactly available.

DETECTIVE MACDONALD: Because he's dead? You killed him and buried the body someplace we'll never find him?

ADAM: No. Maybe he's dead—like, *actually* dead. Let's just say his body is lost and isn't coming back.

DETECTIVE MACDONALD: Lost where, kid?

ADAM: In the rainbow, of course.

DETECTIVE MACDONALD: *(a pause, then laughter)* Well, now I know you've lost your fucking mind. Now, I may look like a patient man, but buddy—I believe your bullshit is pushing me to the end of the line.

ADAM: I'm not joking. The Rainbow Filth. Hauser said it wasn't a drug.

DETECTIVE MACDONALD: No? Then what the fuck was it?

ADAM: *(audible swallowing)* A portal.

When Liz got back from Cambodia, she was changed. I noticed it the second I picked her up from the airport, even though I didn't want to admit it. It was her eyes that gave it away. That, and the way she kissed me. Something happened on the trip—I didn't know what, but I knew one thing; it was Hauser's fault.

My mind traveled to dark territories—of course, the first thing I thought was that she cheated on me with him.

It was the obvious go-to, right? Those first few days back, she was distant. Slept all day. Hardly ate. Which was strange considering how the in-flight meal home was the best thing she'd eaten in the past two weeks. I let it go for the first seventy-two hours, not giving her a hard time because she was exhausted and jetlagged. But on day four, I confronted her.

"So . . . " I said, walking into our apartment's living room with two steaming TV dinners. Meatloaf and mashed potatoes. "Can we talk about the trip?"

She didn't say anything at first. Instead, she focused on the TV, whatever Netflix show was playing at random.

"Liz?"

Finally, her attention swung back to me.

"Did something happen in Cambodia? Something you want to tell me?"

I could see in her eyes that something did happen, but it was nothing she wanted to speak of. "No."

Netflix stole her attention yet again.

"Liz, come on. You can tell me. I promise—whatever it is—you can tell me."

She didn't face me again for the rest of the evening. "I know," was all she said, and I left it at that.

For a little while.

The following morning, I decided to make my stand.

"Hey," I said, the second her eyes fluttered open.

She stretched and yawned, wrapping herself in the sheets like a human burrito. "Hey."

I sat in the corner of the room near the computer desk. The words were hard to say, but they needed to be said. "I hate asking this, *like* this. Feel like I'm ambushing you."

She propped herself up on her elbows. "Then don't."

"Did you cheat on me?"

Her response was a squinty stare, and that was the longest ten seconds of my entire life. "Did I cheat?"

"In Cambodia. With . . . Hauser?"

She rolled her eyes and then her body, off the bed, and

headed into the bathroom. She took the sheets with her to keep her naked body covered, and I knew I was in trouble. (See, whenever we fought, she did this thing where she wouldn't let me see her naked. It was like a punishment of sorts. Eye-rolling, I know.)

Of course, I couldn't let it go. I had the opportunity to stop what was happening, to apologize and backtrack, but I couldn't. Now that it was out there, the accusation, I needed to follow through.

"Liz . . . " I said in that pleading voice, the one I knew she vehemently disliked.

"Don't start with the voice. I fucking hate that voice."

"Just—let's talk it out. You and me. Let's just get it all out there."

"There's nothing to talk about," she snapped.

"Oh, I disagree."

There was a brief pause, and then the bathroom door opened a crack. I saw a single eye peering at me through the slit. "You want to talk about how much of an asshole you are to me?"

"We can if you want."

"You really think I flew around the world just to fuck my college professor?"

I didn't have a good response for that, so I went with, "No, I don't think that."

"Then why'd you bring it up?"

"I . . . " Shame got the best of me, and I hung my head. My cheeks burned with embarrassment and instant regret. "I'm an asshole, you're right. That was dumb of me."

"Yes, it was."

"You've acted differently since you've come home, and I just—"

"Ever think I just needed to acclimate back into the routine of things? I mean, Christ—I was gone two weeks, living in the fucking jungle."

"Yes," I said, raising my hands as if that would deescalate the situation. It was the mime's equivalent to telling her to *calm down*. It just made things worse. "Of course, but . . . I don't know—my gut feels like something happened out there. Something you might want to share with me, that's all. I'm sorry I accused you of cheating. That was super fucked up and wrong, and I take it back."

She paused, leering at me through the space between the door and the jamb. I stuck out my lower lip, pleading for forgiveness.

"Nothing happened out there. It was a waste. A wasted trip, and I regret going. Okay?"

"Okay," I told her. "Just . . . I'm here if you need anything."

"I'm fine," she said, shutting the door. Then she opened it again and added, "Thank you."

We hardly talked the rest of the day, but things did get better after that.

At least . . . for a little while.

A month later and I still couldn't shake the idea that something happened during the Cambodia trip. I became obsessed with finding out the truth, so I went asking questions. I tried Billy and Deana first. They were close friends, and I was pretty sure I could talk to them, get some answers without the details of my visit getting back to Liz. Deana—maybe not so much. She was Liz's best friend after all, her "ride-or-die bitch" (whatever the hell that means), and I couldn't trust she would keep our conversation confidential. But Billy—he'd keep the beans from spilling. I just had to hope I could get him alone and make him promise not to tell anyone, especially Deana.

I visited their apartment on a Tuesday afternoon. Liz had headed back home for the day and was planning to spend the afternoon shopping at the Short Hills Mall with her mother. She'd be back later that evening, but that gave me plenty of time to do some digging.

Billy answered the door on the second knock.

"Hey, man," he greeted me. He was wearing a sleeveless white tee with what looked like a mustard stain near the collar. He had a craft beer can in hand. "Everything all right?"

"I think so," I said, not really sure. Not sure at all. "Deana here?"

"Nah, man. She's out. What's going on?"

"Perfect. Wondering if I could have a word with you."

"Yeah, come on in."

I went in, and he offered me a beer, which I gladly accepted. He drained the rest of his current drink and then grabbed two more out of the fridge, handing one to me. We popped the tops, and he made us clink the cans together, like we were toasting to good times.

Though these were anything but good times.

"Just the guys, hanging out," he said, planting himself on the couch. I took the seat across from him. "We should do this more often, man."

"Oh, yeah. Totally." I didn't want to waste time, so I got right down to business. "Billy, I need to ask you something, and I need you to promise me two things."

He stared at me as any good, concerned friend would. "Sure, man. Anything—you name it."

"I need you to keep this between us. You can't tell Deana. And you can't tell Liz."

"Sure, man. I can keep a secret. Unless . . . you're going to tell me you're about to hurt yourself or something like—"

"It's nothing like that."

"Okay," he shrugged, as if to say, *let's do this. Make with the secrets.* "What's the second thing?"

"Huh? Oh, I was counting Deana and Liz as two separate things."

"Ha, okay."

"It's hard to say out loud, but . . . Cambodia."

Billy flicked up his eyebrows. "Yeah, figured that's where you were headed with this."

"Something happened there, didn't it?"

He glanced over his shoulder for his second, a short, nuanced movement, as if there was someone in the next room potentially listening in. I turned toward the hallway and didn't get a sense that the apartment was occupied by anyone but us.

"Some things happened there, yes. Not sure if I'm at liberty to say *what*, though."

"I just need to know . . . " I swallowed. I don't know why—it was almost harder to ask Billy than it was Liz directly. "Liz—did she . . . cheat on me?"

At this, Billy flinched. "What? No, man. Why . . . why would you think that?"

His answer stunned me. Honestly, I expected him to admit that Liz had been with Hauser, that the two of them had gotten together and been at it for a while now. But he admitted no such thing, and, in fact, his face maintained a genuine sturdiness to it. In other words, I believed he was telling me the truth.

"She's been acting different since you all got back. Distant. Cold. Just . . . *off*. Not herself."

Billy's eyes fell on his beer. For a silent spell, he watched the aluminum can as if he was giving the inanimate object a chance to speak. Then: "I can't tell you everything about what happened . . . but I'll tell you this— whatever Liz saw there, it spooked her."

"Spooked her?" I shook my head. "I thought you guys were going on a getaway. Hiking and outdoorsy stuff."

"That's true. But that's not the only thing we went there for."

"Well . . . what else?" I didn't need to ask—I already knew. Or suspected. "Was it drugs?"

He dipped his head in a sorrowful nod. "Yeah, man. It was drugs all right. The motherlode. The very thing Hauser has been searching his entire life for. Well, not his *entire* life. But at least the past few years."

"What drug?" *Christ,* did I even want to know? A part of me thought this was enough, as far as I needed to dig.

Liz had a bad trip and that was it. But something in Billy's eyes made me thirst for more answers. "What drug, Billy? What did you guys do out there in the jungle?"

"Have you ever heard of . . . the Rainbow Filth?" he asked.

Puzzled, I told him, "No."

He didn't seem surprised. "There's a river just south of Vietnam that runs through Cambodia, and it has no name. The locals have a name for it, but the closest thing in English it translates to is *The Rainbow Filth*."

"Has a lovely ring to it."

"If you look at the surface of the water at the right angle when the sun hits it just so, you can see this rainbow sheen atop it, like an oil spill when the light hits it just right. Glitters like diamonds, if the diamonds were made of some crystalline Lucky Charms."

"Delicious. Now I want Lucky Charms."

Billy didn't appreciate my attempt to lighten the mood. His face grew dark and serious, and there was no stopping him now. "The river is said to contain certain chemical properties akin to LSD, only . . . much more potent. And much more mystical."

I wanted to do a spooky voice, *Oooooh* and *Aaaaaah*, but I refrained. I half-thought he was putting me on, that this was all some big gag—or a ploy to cover up the truth: that Liz *was* cheating on me.

But then again—Liz's previous point had some weight. Why would she travel to the opposite side of the globe just to fuck her college professor when she could have easily done the dirty back home. And if that were true, if she had gone there to cheat, why take her friends along for the unfaithful excursion, opening up the possibility of them narcing on her later. Didn't add up.

"So, what?" I asked, trying to hide my skepticism. "You all drank from the river, got really sick, and saw some fucked up shit?"

He stared at me for enough time to pass where I felt

uncomfortable. Like I'd said something offensive and the silence, the moment to sit there with my guilt and shame, was my punishment.

"Something like that," he said, and I noticed a bead of sweat dripping from his prematurely receding hairline. "You can't ingest the river. That will just make you sick."

"Well . . . how do you take it then? Turkey baster up the ass?"

"No, Adam," he said, somewhat disgusted. "There's a method, but . . . look, it doesn't matter. You have to find the right place in the river in order to achieve the proper effect."

"What do you mean? Like, if you take the stuff from one end of the river, you'll have a different experience than if you took it from the other?"

"That's exactly what I mean—except one experience will leave you seriously ill and the other . . . well, the other is quite literally out of this world."

I cocked an eyebrow. "Not sure I follow."

"The properties that make up the Rainbow Filth have been said to have the ability to transport the user to another plane of existence."

"Uh . . . okay." Sounded ludicrous, but honestly, what else was I expecting? "So, like, mentally or . . . "

"It has the ability to change the chemical properties in your brain, unlocking a secret door to another dimension."

"Sooooo . . . mentally."

"The door can be opened, and you can step through to the other side."

"Sooooo, just so we're clear. You're talking about physically stepping through a door into another dimension?"

"Precisely."

"Wow. That's . . . that's impossible. You realize that, right?"

Billy snorted as if to say, *I wish that was the truth.*

I kept my composure, though I wanted to call him a

lunatic, question him, and understand why he believed in such nonsense. "It just doesn't make sense."

"Thought the same thing," he said, cracking his knuckles, "when Hauser told us about it. But then I saw it with my own eyes."

"What do you mean?"

"Hauser . . . he found the Rainbow Filth, took it, and stepped through the door."

"And you watched him?"

"Yes."

"Did you take it too?"

"No," he said, shaking his head, "but your girlfriend did."

After Billy's admission, he sort of clammed up regarding the topic of taking a mysterious psychedelic substance with the supernatural ability to open doors to an alternate world. *I don't want to talk about it* became his go-to catchphrase, along with, *Maybe you should just ask Liz what happened.* I tried to press him, but he gave me nothing. Before I left, he even tried to walk back some of what he told me, stating that, "Maybe I didn't know what I saw. I was hungry and sleep-deprived when it happened, so my memory of things is a little hazy. I was also taking edibles nonstop, so there's that."

I left the apartment with more questions than answers. But from what I gathered, at least Liz wasn't cheating on me. At least not with Hauser. At least, I didn't think so. I believed them for now, but now I had to deal with the second part of this issue—she was experimenting with some wild drugs, truly dangerous stuff, and I wasn't sure I was okay with that. As previously stated, hard drugs were not my thing. Clearly, she was beginning to develop a taste. Possibly an addiction.

And it was Hauser's fault, right? His influence on her had become a source of irritation, the kind that buries itself deep into an open wound you never knew you had. I knew I'd have to confront the bastard head-on, and I would. But first—I needed more information.

I needed the truth.

I decided to visit the Hurt twins.

Recording

Property of the
Shrewsbury Police

Saturday/June 2nd, 2024/7:39 p.m.
Interviewing Detective: Chase MacDonald
Witness/Suspect: Adam Godfrey

DETECTIVE MACDONALD: Back up a second. You're trying to tell me that this cat believed his college professor drank some magic fucking potion from some dirty-ass river near Vietnam, and what? A magic door opened in the middle of the jungle? He stepped through it like some wardrobe-into-Narnia bullshit?

ADAM: That's what it sounded like at the time, yes.

DETECTIVE MACDONALD: This is getting absurd.

ADAM: I know!

DETECTIVE MACDONALD: I feel like you're lying to me. This whole story reeks of utter nonsense and lies, and I want it to start making some goddamn sense. Or I swear to God, I'll make sure we pin this whole clusterfuck on you and you alone. I'll make sure you go down for murdering that professor and your little girlfriend.

ADAM: You know you have no proof—nothing

that will hold up in court. Your only chance of solving this thing is to listen to me. And to believe me.

DETECTIVE MACDONALD: *(sighing)* I'm a normal man, Godfrey. I believe in simple things. Sure, I go to church on Sundays, listen to the sermons. I understand that ninety-nine percent of the stories we hear from the Bible are nothing more than parables and metaphors, anecdotes to convey some lesson we can take with us to lead better lives. Hell, maybe it's even a hundred percent bullshit. Not sure I believe in God in the traditional sense at all, but shit—it makes me feel good going and sitting in that church every Sunday with my wife and kids next to me. Provides comfort. God might not exist, the Devil might not exist, and Jesus could just be some literary character, no more real than Captain Ahab or Ebenezer Scrooge. Yet, I sit and listen and, on some level—I believe. And my point is, Godfrey, I don't believe a lick of the nonsense you're spewing at me. Not a lick. Understand?

ADAM: You don't have to believe me yet. You just have to listen. Because when you deal with what comes next, what comes after our conversation . . . you'll want to heed my advice.

DETECTIVE MACDONALD: And what advice might that be?

ADAM: *(audibly swallowing)* Don't go looking for them. Whatever you do, don't fucking look for them.

I met with the Hurt twins the next day. They were in their dorm's common room, sitting on the end cushions of the three-seat sofa opposite each other. Russell was reading from a Russian Lit textbook, jotting notes in a spiral notepad. Arthur was playing solitaire. The cards were spread out before him and he was lazily adding to the chains below the stacks of what remained of the deck. Both looked hungover as fuck.

"Fellas," I said, knocking on the open door.

They peeked up, saw it was me, and then simultaneously grunted. My presence clearly wasn't welcomed, but they didn't kick me out either.

"Billy told us you'd be stopping by," Russell said with zero enthusiasm. This was news to me; I hadn't clued Billy into my plans. "Said you'd be asking about . . . the *trip*."

Hated the way he spoke the word *trip*. His tone dripped with aggravation.

Russell added, "We won't tell you anything you don't already know."

Some people passed in the hallway behind me, snickering and joking and having fun. I wished I was having fun. I kicked the rock that propped open the door, relieving it from its post. The hydraulic closer hissed, and the door eased shut.

"Oh, look at this," Russell said, putting down the notebook and closing the textbook. "Loverboy is trying to intimidate us."

An amused grin spread across Arthur's face.

"I know you guys don't know me at all," I said as I leaned against the wall and crossed my arms, "but I'm begging you for some answers here."

"We told her she shouldn't have gone in," Arthur said, still grinning. "She didn't listen." He went back to solitaire, placing the seven of hearts beneath the eight of spades.

"Stop," Russell said to his brother. "We promised

Hauser we wouldn't talk about it." He seemed generally upset that his twin had let that tidbit slip.

"Oh, brother. Come on. Look at the kid. He's confused. And obviously very determined to make sense of this."

I bit my cheek just enough to feel some pain. "I just want to know if Liz will be alright."

Arthur shot me a knowing smile. "Define 'all right.' "

"You know what I mean." I wanted to crack both their heads together. "Does the drug have any lasting effect? Did she say anything to you? Anything at all?"

"Why are you asking us?" Russell snapped. "I mean, shouldn't you be asking her? Hauser himself?"

Silence.

Then Arthur said, "Oh shit—she doesn't know that you know, and you don't want her to know."

"Very good," I said.

"What if we tell her?" Russell said, a clear attempt to get under my skin. It worked. The kid's tone knew how to burrow.

"Go ahead."

He snorted.

Arthur continued with his solo card game but didn't check out of the conversation. His eyes alternated between me and the puzzle before him. "I'll tell you what you want to know."

Russell whipped his head toward his brother. "Arth—"

"Easy, brother. It's no big deal. After all, how much do we really know?"

A tense moment passed, but Russell ended up sighing, an exaggerated breath that took several seconds to complete. Then he got up and left the common room.

"Touchy he is," Arthur said, impersonating a miniature green character from a popular film franchise.

"Seems like a real gem," I said, leaving the less-than-comfortable position on the wall. "I just want to know what happened to Liz. She won't speak to me about it."

"She'll never speak of it. No one will because . . . " He

paused, trying to find the right way to convey what he'd experienced. "Because we're not really sure what happened."

"What about this drug—The Rainbow Filth?"

He acknowledged the drug's existence with a brief nod. "So Billy spilled those beans, huh? Didn't tell us that on the phone. Just that you'd be by to ask questions. God, I wish he hadn't said anything."

"Well, he did. So now I'm aware of certain things."

"Did he tell you about Liz?"

"That she took it."

He sucked his teeth. "Yeah she did."

"And this door?"

"Door? Is that what Billy called it?"

"It's the term he used."

Arthur shifted in his seat as if the cushion had thumb tacks poking out of it. "Ah, well, I guess that's one word for it."

"What would you call it?"

He gathered his thoughts for a beat. My restless leg pumped incessantly while I waited for him to explain this craziness. "They call it the *Rainbow* Filth not just for the prismatic quality in the river. When it's in your bloodstream, you literally see in rainbows. So I'm told."

"You see in rainbows?"

"Yes," he said, keeping a straight face. If he was fibbing, I couldn't tell. "The door is a rainbow. And you follow it to the end."

"And the end is . . . what? A passage to an alternate dimension?"

"Don't know. To my knowledge, there have only been three people to have experienced it. Two of them you know."

"And the third?"

"Man by the name of Walter Bogie." *Bow-gee.* I'd never heard the name before.

"Who's that?"

"Someone Hauser went to school with twenty years ago. It's how he first learned of the drug."

"Where is he now?"

He shrugged. "No clue. Sore subject for Hauser."

"Did Liz say anything to you guys? Did she . . . *fuck*. Did she say anything about what she saw?"

He stared at me, his lips shrinking. "No. She's been very quiet. But whatever she saw after taking the drug, it . . . let's just say it didn't agree with her." His shoulders bounced as if to say, *Oh well, that's how it goes sometimes*. "She had a bad trip, man."

"She's said nothing?"

"Not to me." His grin reinstated itself. "The only one who truly knows what happened that day is Hauser, man."

"Where can I find him?"

"He's available after his lectures. There's one tomorrow night."

"You think Liz will be there?"

He kicked the thought around. "Doubtful, man. I don't want to say the two had a falling out after Cambodia, but let's say they're not as close as they once were."

This, of all things, made me the happiest.

"One more thing," I said, creeping toward the door, prepping to make a swift exit. I was starting to feel suffocated in here. "Hauser and Liz—they ever hook up? That you know of?"

At this, he laughed. "I don't know, man. They were close, but I never got the impression the two were playing hide-the-salami behind your back."

I nodded. Thanked him. Then I saw myself out.

Before I could make it down the hallway, he poked his head out of the room.

"Hey, Adam," he said. I turned around. "Be careful with Hauser."

"What do you mean?"

"The guy—I don't think he's *right*."

"Can you elaborate?"

40

"Not really," Arthur Hurt said. "Just . . . you'll see what I mean once you start asking him about the trip. Just . . . be careful is all I'm saying."

And then he closed the door.

Recording

Property of the
Shrewsbury Police

Saturday/June 2nd, 2024/7:59 p.m.
Interviewing Detective: Chase MacDonald
Witness/Suspect: Adam Godfrey

DETECTIVE MACDONALD: So, tell me you went
to visit Hauser after his lecture.

ADAM: I went to visit Hauser after his
lecture.

DETECTIVE MACDONALD: And how'd that go?

ADAM: It was . . . interesting.

DETECTIVE MACDONALD: Care to fucking
expand on that?

(knock at door, door squeaking open)

DETECTIVE CARLA ROBINSON: Hey, Chase.
Your wife is on line one.

DETECTIVE MACDONALD: Shiiiit. Okay, tell
her I'll be there in two seconds.

DETECTIVE CARLA ROBINSON: You want me to
have someone sit in with him?

DETECTIVE MACDONALD: No, Adam here will
be a good boy. Won't you, kid?

ADAM: Best behavior. Scout's honor.

(chair leg scraping against ground)

DETECTIVE MACDONALD: I'll be back in five. Take a breather. When I get back, we get to Hauser and what happened that night. Understood?

ADAM: Oh yes. I can't wait to tell you what happened that night. It's my favorite part of the story.

(door shuts)

(silence for three minutes and thirty-nine seconds)

ADAM: *(incoherent whispering)*

(silence for twelve seconds)

ADAM: *(continued incoherent whispering)*

(silence for fifteen seconds)

ADAM: *(whispering)* I know . . . I know . . . don't worry . . . you worry too much . . . I won't tell them . . . promise . . . I would never . . . *(incoherent)* . . . stop it . . . you can't . . . we made a deal . . . but you promised . . . *(louder)* you promised! You—

(door opens)

(footsteps)

DETECTIVE MACDONALD: Adam? Who were you talking to?

ADAM: What?

DETECTIVE MACDONALD: I heard you talking as I was walking in here. Thought you said 'you promised?'

ADAM: I didn't say anything.

DETECTIVE MACDONALD: Are you okay? You look . . . unwell.

ADAM: I'm fine.

DETECTIVE MACDONALD: You sure, kid? I was only gone for a couple of minutes, and you look like you were visited by a ghost.

ADAM: *(angry)* I said I'm fine.

DETECTIVE MACDONALD: Okay. *(chair scraping against floor)* You want to tell me what happened when you went to go visit Hauser?

ADAM: Sure.

DETECTIVE MACDONALD: You sure you're okay? We can take a minute if you want. Told the wife I'd be coming home late, not to wait up. So I got all night.

ADAM: No, I'm fine. I'll finish the story.

DETECTIVE MACDONALD: Fine, fine. But you know you're being recorded, and we can listen to the playback later, so if you did want to tell us anything, any conversation you may have been having with yourself while I was gone . . . now would be a good time to speak up.

ADAM: I'm. Fine.

DETECTIVE MACDONALD: Okay, hotshot. I believe you. The floor is yours.

ADAM: As I was saying . . . my next stop was to visit Hauser and get to the bottom of what happened in Cambodia . . . what

happened to Liz . . . what she saw there
in the Rainbow Filth . . .

The night before I planned to visit Hauser, Liz and I went to sleep like normal. We ate pizza for dinner, enjoyed a glass of white wine each, and then watched old episodes of *Scrubs* (our favorite show) before getting to the bedroom and climbing into bed. I tried to put some moves on her, but she wasn't having it, told me the pizza had upset her stomach and there would be no lovemaking this evening, not even a quickie. I kissed her forehead and told her that was fine, that I wasn't in the mood either, which was partly a lie. I had been in the mood, had been ever since she'd come home from her two-week excursion. We hadn't had sex since before she left, and the few times we tried, she tapped out before things got started, citing one excuse or another. Of course, this only furthered my concern for her, since, before her trip, her sexual appetite had been on par with mine.

But I let it all go, didn't press her on the topic. I didn't press her on anything. Instead I waited, biding my time until the opportunity presented itself. Until all the facts were discovered. Until I knew the truth. This was a delicate situation, and before I could go to Liz with all the information I had gathered, I needed to speak with Hauser directly.

She fell asleep right away, and I couldn't get there. I tossed and turned for a solid two hours. Sometime around midnight, I heard her whispering in her sleep. I couldn't decipher what she was saying or who the words were directed at, but she seemed to be in distress. Whatever dream she had formed in her unconscious mind was quickly trespassing into nightmarish territories. I toyed with the idea of waking her up but didn't. Partly because I was curious and wondering if her muttering would start making sense. Partly because I thought the nightmare phase would pass, and she would go back to dreaming normal dreams.

It went on for a solid fifteen minutes.

I watched.

At one point, when the nightmare reached its horrifying peak, she opened her eyes and stared up at me. Her eyes were so wide I thought they might fall out of their sockets. Even though she appeared to be awake, I could tell she wasn't. A misty glaze clouded her eyes, and I could see she wasn't looking directly *at* me, but *through* me.

"I see them," she said in a strangled voice. Like someone had their hands around her throat, squeezing her vocal cords shut so only the slightest amount of air could pass through. *"I see them at the end of the rainbow."*

And then she turned over and drifted off to sleep.

She didn't make a sound the rest of the night. I know this because I couldn't shut my eyes after that.

Hauser's lecture ended around nine-thirty, and I waited another forty-five minutes for the sycophants and other interested parties to filter out of the hall. We'd made eye contact before that, and he knew the exact reason I was here, gave me a subtle nod like he was expecting this all along. In fact, I understood this subtle acknowledgment to mean he assumed this forthcoming discussion would have happened sooner.

And it should have. Might have saved me some trouble. Might have saved us some lives. It's funny to think about the chain of events, how things unfold, reflect on specific moments where you could have done things slightly differently. If you'd done A instead of B, how would things have played out? Impossible to know for sure, but the thought is always there, haunting me like a spirit stuck in some earthly purgatory.

After the last soul wandered out, Hauser turned to me and motioned for me to follow. We ended up back in his office, which was quite sizable for a lowkey college professor who began his career as an adjunct; it was much too lavish for someone of his tenure. The kind of office the dean might have. He waved his hand for me to have a seat, and I said I'd rather stand, which was true, but also, I didn't want to acquiesce to any of his offers or requests because I didn't want to seem weak. If I took that seat, it would be like submitting to him, his will. There was a game of power being played between us, and he had the upper hand. For one, he held all the knowledge. There were our societal roles to consider as well. He was a prestigious (apparently) professor, and I was just a lowly student, nothing more than a statistic in the university's eyes. If it came to it, if I had to get the university's administration or the police involved, these were things that Hauser had in his back pocket. Like holding a pair of aces against any two random cards. Me? I was trying to see the river with seven-deuce off-suited.

I was getting ahead of myself, though. I came here for answers first. The consequences of Hauser's shitty and illegal behavior would come later.

"Scotch?" he asked, pouring himself a glass.

I preferred a glass of turpentine over anything in Hauser's cabinet, so I politely declined.

"Suit yourself," he said, sipping from the glass and then breathing a sigh of relief, as if the alcohol provided immediate results. He swirled the ice cubes around the bottom of the glass with graceful revolutions. "So . . . I'm guessing you're here to talk about Cambodia?"

"The twins tip you off?"

"You've been to see the twins?" He smiled, pretending he didn't know. But there was no way they *didn't* alert him of my visit. "You're an impressive detective, you know that?"

"Listen—I just want to know what happened out there. The truth. And I want to know . . . " My eyes faltered. I couldn't speak the words aloud, as if by doing so, I was betraying Liz, her trust in me.

"You want to know if I fucked your girlfriend?" His eyes reflected like shiny dimes. His elastic smile shrunk and widened as if his face didn't know how to convey his emotions, whether he wanted to feel pity for me or laugh his ass off. "I didn't fuck your girlfriend, Godfrey."

I shot him an *Are you sure about that?* look.

"I mean, I totally would have," he continued, "if she'd been interested—I'm not above admitting that. She's hot, Godfrey. Not ashamed to say it. And I don't believe that students and professors can't . . . well, have a bit of fun."

Even though admitting he hadn't been with Liz brought some relief, he might as well have told me he did—I wanted to punch a hole through the greasy slimeball's chest all the same.

"What?" He cocked his head back and laughed. "Come on—man-to-man, if you were in my position, what would you do?"

"I don't know, but not that."

"You're naïve, Godfrey. You don't see the world as I have seen it."

"I'm glad you brought that up. In Cambodia, what *did* you guys see?"

At this, he studied me. Sipped from his glass. His eyes guarded secrets, secrets I wanted in on. I was glad Liz wasn't cheating on me, but I needed to know what was going on with her. What was eating at her dreams in the middle of the night, what kind of cancerous mindfuck she'd brought home with her from that stupid trip she never should have gone on in the first place.

"I've been told you've heard the stories of the river, the Rainbow Filth?" He leaned against the cabinet behind him. "You know what it is?"

"A psychedelic from what I gather."

"Yes, traces of the naturally-forming chemical property can be found in the nameless river. An old friend of mine, Water Bogie, went there about twenty years ago. He claimed that he had found the source, experienced it, and ascended to that open doorway that led to the other side. But . . . I never believed him. I begged him to take me there, to find the river and bring back samples, so I too could experience the magic that this place offers. But . . . "

I waited for him to come back from whatever memory currently held him, but he never did until I said, "But?"

"But he refused. Our relationship deteriorated along with his mental health. Killed himself less than a year later."

"Sorry to hear that," I said with little enthusiasm.

"Thank you," he said with the same level of warmth. "I never gave up though. I went to the region several times over the years, interviewed the indigenous people, stayed with them and learned what they knew of the river and the power it contained, which was surprisingly very little. Finally . . . finally I found it. The source."

"And that's why you went there with your students?"

"They offered their assistance once they heard about the magic it contained, the once in a lifetime opportunity that only one other person on the planet had experienced."

"And that person killed himself, presumably *because* of the drug?" I was starting to get pissed at Liz for even entertaining the thought, let alone going on the trip. But what was in the past had passed, and there was nothing to be done about it now. The only thing that mattered was that she would not suffer the same fate as this Walter Bogie guy. "You people are . . . "

"Are what?" he challenged. I got the sense he was willing to get physical if the situation called for it—the way he puffed his chest, chewed the insides of his cheeks, and the way he leered at me so contemptuously. Like if I said the wrong thing, he'd flip the desk at me. This alpha-male-macho bullshit didn't fly with me, and I held my ground. "Pioneers of a level of consciousness that could only be imagined?"

"I was going to say delusional wackos, but sure—that works too." It felt good to stand up to this asshole, feed him his own bullshit.

"You don't understand. You will never understand."
Then his lips formed a smile, the kind inspired by some
enlightened idea. "Unless . . . you want to."

"What are you saying? If you're trying to sign me up
for your next expedition to Cambodia, you can stick that
straight up your ass and bend it sideways, pal."

A hearty chuckle escaped him. "You're a little bit of a
cunt, aren't you, Godfrey? Okay. So here's what I'm
thinking . . . "

"Ohhhh. You're thinking now? Could have fooled me."

He let the comment go, and I could tell by the way his
eyes darkened that he wouldn't suffer much more of my
backtalk. Not finishing his thought right away, he strolled
over to the cabinet behind his desk and opened it, sighing
as if what he was about to reveal was some last-ditch effort
to appease me. When he turned around to face me, he was
carrying a mason jar about the size of a two-liter soda
bottle. A dark, viscous liquid sat at the bottom of the glass,
several inches thick. At least, I thought it was liquid. As he
set down the jar, I noticed the liquid was moving and not
in a sloshing around sort of way. Like, it was *climbing*. I
watched in awe as the contents ascended the side of the
glass facing me. I tried to interpret what I was seeing, like
some optical trick performed by an illusionist; I was trying
to figure it out before it could be explained to me.

"The fuck?" I said out loud, though I hadn't meant to.

"Pretty, aren't they?" Hauser admired the things as
they stretched for the jar's closed lid.

"What . . . " But then I realized exactly *what* they were.
I'd never seen one in real life before, only in movies and
textbooks with pictures in them.

Leeches.

The fat, dark slugs roused out of whatever coma they'd
been in. Great climbers they were, they began to scale the
sides of their see-through containment pod. One of them
was already at the roof of the mason jar, seeking a way out.
Breathing holes had been drilled through the top.

"Pulled these suckers from the river, the exact spot where the Rainbow Filth runs through. These little fellas are my pride and joy."

I remembered how Billy said you couldn't drink the water, that ingesting the Filth would only make you sick.

Suddenly . . . it clicked. As inhabitants of the river, the leeches contained the Filth, and letting them feed from you released a certain amount of the toxin into the bloodstream—enough, but not enough to poison you.

Hauser confirmed this. "It's a beautiful side effect."

"I'd call it disgusting."

"We're planning another *trip,*" he said abruptly, disregarding my reaction to the slimy critters. I didn't ask what he planned on keeping them for, didn't prod—he volunteered the information, and I was amazed he had.

"What?"

"Relax. It will be more controlled this time. Here. In Pennsylvania, near Gettysburg. There's a field out there where we can take the drug. We'll have someone overseeing our journey, a doctor that I am very good friends with—a professor at the university. She'll sit in and ensure the safety of everyone involved."

Everyone involved.

Liz?

"Before you ask," Hauser said, reveling in the fact that I was on edge and mighty angry with him, with Liz, with Walter Bogie, with everyone who'd ever had anything to do with the Rainbow Filth. "Yes, Liz is coming. And no, I didn't invite her. She insisted."

I almost lunged at him. "You fuck."

"Relax, Godfrey." He pumped his hand as if that would calm me. "You're not the boss of her. You can't tell her what to do, how to feel. She wants this. More than me. Well, maybe not *more*, but her appetite for a knowledge that transcends our own consciousnesses is parallel with my own."

"I won't let her go. I'll strap her to the fucking bedposts before I let you take her."

He tilted back his head, projecting rip-roaring laughter at the ceiling. "Oh, Godfrey. You're too cute. Let me tell you something about your girlfriend—she's determined. And a determined woman cannot be messed with, impeded upon, or derailed." He sighed as if the proceeding knowledge bomb fatigued him. "In short—she will do this with or without your consent."

"We'll see about that."

"But there's an alternative."

"Oh? Can't wait to hear it."

"You can come with."

A bolt of surprise struck me, and I felt dizzy in the aftermath. "Come with?"

"Participate. Take the Filth with us. Accompany us on our journey to worlds unknown."

I bit my lip, resisting the urge to take that mason jar and jam those leeches down his throat. "You think I'm stupid? After telling me the only person, before you and Liz taking the drug, killed himself, and with Liz acting super weird lately . . . you want me to fucking join you?"

"It's the only way Liz will come back from what she's seen. To experience it again. To know what the Filth knows."

Maybe that's the problem, I thought. *Maybe she's experienced too much.*

"You seem normal, though," I said, an accusation more than it was a statement. "You seem like the same asshole you were when I first met you."

Another amused laugh. "Well, I didn't go where Liz went."

"And where did she go?"

"Beyond."

"What the fuck does that even mean?"

"It's something that can't be accurately explained, I'm afraid." He winked at me and I never needed a shower so badly in my life. "You'll just have to experience it yourself."

My jaw ached from grinding my teeth together. "When's the trip?"

"This Saturday."
Five days.
"Bus leaves at noon," he added.
I told him I'd fucking be there.

Recording

Property of the
Shrewsbury Police

Saturday/June 2nd, 2024/8:36 p.m.
Interviewing Detective: Chase MacDonald
Witness/Suspect: Adam Godfrey

DETECTIVE MACDONALD: This Saturday, meaning last Saturday? Right?

ADAM: That's correct. We're finally getting to the final showdown. All the pieces have fallen into place.

DETECTIVE MACDONALD: Well, it's about damn time.

ADAM: Just trying to be thorough, Detective. I wouldn't want to leave anything out that you might go asking about later. So you can't accuse me of hiding certain facts. I want to lay all the cards on the table. So there's no confusion.

DETECTIVE MACDONALD: I'm plenty confused. I mean, poisonous leeches with psychedelic side effects—you don't expect me to believe this, do you?

ADAM: I'm not expecting anything. I'm telling you what happened. Whether you believe it or not is not really up to me.

DETECTIVE MACDONALD: Great. Well, for your sake, the last part of this story better be pretty fucking convincing, because right now, the way I see it, you killed Hauser and all your little idiot friends, and hid their bodies somewhere in the mountains.

ADAM: Haven't found them yet, though. That's the problem with your theory.

DETECTIVE MACDONALD: We'll find them.

ADAM: If they're there.

DETECTIVE MACDONALD: . . . Correct.

ADAM: And if they're not?

DETECTIVE MACDONALD: I think you need to quit playing mind games with me and tell me about last Saturday. Lewis Hauser and his cult of drug-worshipping hipsters are getting on a bus with a mason jar full of leeches and heading to the country, so they can get hopped up on the magic sauce and take a magic carpet ride to some fucking alternate dimension. That about sum it up?

ADAM: Yes. But you forgot Annabelle Gump.

DETECTIVE MACDONALD: Who in the blue fuck is that?

ADAM: The other professor that Hauser mentioned. She was there to . . . *control* the situation.

DETECTIVE MACDONALD: Why do you say it like that?

ADAM: She was a weird woman. Hardly spoke a word. And after knowing her for about five minutes, I don't think she was a professor. Or a doctor for that matter. She had this head of long, dirty gray hair that was all knotted and starting to dreadlock. She wore an all-black dress with wrist frills. She looked more like a witch doctor than an actual one.

DETECTIVE MACDONALD: And this woman . . . she never spoke a word?

ADAM: A few. When the ceremony began.

DETECTIVE MACDONALD: Ceremony? I'm sorry, the fuck?

ADAM: We got off Hauser's bus and went to the campsite he'd marked out on the map. It was out in the middle of nowhere—you know where it is. I already gave you the coordinates.

DETECTIVE MACDONALD: We know where it is.

ADAM: There were logs set up in a circle, one for each of us. I sat next to Liz of course. (subtle laugh) I remember trying to reach out for her hand, like I should have that day when I first met Hauser, but she ignored me. She was ignoring me a lot in the days before. Especially after she tried to convince me not to go. Begged me to leave it alone. She even broke up with me.

DETECTIVE MACDONALD: She broke up with you?

ADAM: Told me straight up to 'stay the fuck out of my'—her—'life.'

DETECTIVE MACDONALD: Rough.

ADAM: But I couldn't. I felt . . . responsible for her, you know? She was in trouble. I had to save her. And going with her to this . . . whatever it was—it was the only way I could. Save her, I mean. If I was there with her, experiencing what she was. Maybe I could understand it too. Maybe it would make sense and maybe when it was over, things would return to normal. *(a huge sigh)* Anyway, after Hauser distributed the leeches, one apiece, the woman entered the center of the circle and lit a fire with a small bundle of sticks that had been arranged before we got there. Hauser instructed us to put the leeches on the soft spot of our arms near the elbow joint, where you get blood drawn. We did as he told us, and I could feel the little bastard latch on. Hauser must have been starving the parasites because it went to town on my arm. It contracted and expanded with each suck, the slimy surface of its skin undulating with each take.

DETECTIVE MACDONALD: That's gross, kid.

ADAM: It was gross. I wanted to rip the thing off. But I didn't. I remember looking over at Liz, her face. Her eyes were closed. She was biting her lip. Similar to the way she did when she orgasmed.

DETECTIVE MACDONALD: Okay, spare me the details of your girlfriend's orgasm. Please. I mean, what the fuck, man?

ADAM: It's important to know, for the record, that the beginning of the experience was almost like a climax itself.

DETECTIVE MACDONALD: And why the fuck is that important?

ADAM: Because it was all downhill from there.

Annabelle Gump started to chant when I felt the effects take hold. Nonsense things, a language I could not decipher, if it was a real human language at all. Imagine syllables of different words spoken at random with no flow or rhythm.

After the rush of what I could only call *the first wave*, my mind evened out. Day became dusk all-too-quickly. The world smelled of some earthly odor, wet mud mixed with freshly mutilated grass. I realized my vision was hazy, but then saw that was because Annabelle had a pot over the small fire and the substance within was generating a considerable cloud of thick smoke. The twins were high right off the bat, giggling and holding their stomachs as if they hurt from the laughter. Liz swayed on her log, like the earth below her was a choppy sea amid a fierce storm. I wanted to reach out and hug her, but whatever the leech had released into my bloodstream kept me rooted.

Annabelle continued to chant. Then she said in plain English: "The rainbow world is coming." Then she looked directly at me and spoke words I will never, ever forget: "Prepare your eyes for the new color."

No idea what it meant at the time, but clarity was coming soon, and I felt it, the oncoming effect palpable-like. I saw the leech had abandoned its pursuit of my blood. During the first wave, it must have gotten fat on my ichor and decided to take a break. Where it went, I never did find out. But the leech was gone, and I examined the arms of the five others, and their leeches had also absconded from the scene of the crime.

We sat in stasis for quite a while. Not sure what I was expecting to come next, but what happened . . . well, it was out of this world.

Literally.

The world melted for a second. Have you ever seen a reel of film get caught in a projector and burn on screen? How the material bubbles and warps for about three seconds before all you can see is the pure-white square from the intense glow of the projector's bulb? That's what happened to our minds when we entered *the second wave*. Our vision melted, bubbled and popped, and there was a brief moment of white space that occupied our vision—I'm speaking from my experience, but I assume the others took the same journey. It's important to note that.

When the world came back from that pure white element, it was changed. Not the landscape so much. The field was there, and so were the trees and the mountains near the horizon. But the *colors* had changed. It was no longer just before dark. There was this rainbow aurora that had dropped over the world, filled it like an Instagram filter. It moved before us as if the glow of this place was alive, a sentient force that realized our presence. Amoeba-like in the way it stretched across the invisible highways it traveled along.

Then, in the near distance, we spotted it. The very thing we'd come for. Access to that *other* place.

Hauser was the first to move toward it.

"Go forth," Annabelle encouraged us, as if she could see the thing too, even though she hadn't taken any of the Filth. "Go forth and discover what this place has in store for you."

So we did. Like a parade of stoners shuffling toward their favorite 7-Eleven for munchies, we ambled toward the door that rested in the center of the field, a bright light shining from behind it, a whitish glow outlining all four edges as if God Himself and the Heavens He called home were waiting on the other side.

I followed Hauser. Liz. The Twins. Billy and Deana.

Hauser opened the door and let the light fill our vision. Then, one at a time, we stepped on through.

Recording

Property of the Shrewsbury Police

Saturday/June 2nd, 2024/8:59 p.m.
Interviewing Detective: Chase MacDonald
Witness/Suspect: Adam Godfrey

DETECTIVE MACDONALD: I think we're done for the night.

ADAM: Are you sure? We're just getting to the juicy parts. The stuff you *really* want to know about. The secrets.

DETECTIVE MACDONALD: Been doing this a long time, kid. I know how this story ends.

ADAM: Oh, I really don't think you do.

DETECTIVE MACDONALD: Listen, this isn't the first time a bunch of druggies filled themselves up with some crazy chemical and then went frolicking in the woods. I know the sequence of events—one of them has a bad trip, thinks his friends are demons coming to collect his soul or some goofy shit, then ends up killing them out of fear. Heard it, don't need to hear it again.

ADAM: That's no way to be, Detective.

You've been asking for this story all night. I'm so close to finishing it. Don't you want to know what was beyond the door?

DETECTIVE MACDONALD: I'd rather you tell me the goddamn truth. How you killed your friends and where you put their bodies.

ADAM: I didn't kill them.

DETECTIVE MACDONALD: Come on.

ADAM: I didn't fucking kill them! (*fist pounds desk*)

DETECTIVE MACDONALD: All right, hotshot. No need to get angry. I'm just tired. And I need more coffee. You need more coffee?

ADAM: No . . .

DETECTIVE MACDONALD: Okay. I'm getting more coffee. And when I come back, you finish this story. You tell me what happened, the truth—and no more talk about doorways to other worlds. Got it?

ADAM: But that's what happened. I saw it with my own eyes.

DETECTIVE MACDONALD: I'm sure you did. But it . . . it wasn't real, kid. It was whatever you poisoned yourself with.

ADAM: It was real. I know it was.

DETECTIVE MACDONALD: And how do you know that?

ADAM: Because . . .

DETECTIVE MACDONALD: 'Because' isn't an answer, numb skull.

ADAM: Because I still have its mark on me.

DETECTIVE MACDONALD: What are you talking about?

ADAM: The thing we found . . . it's marked me. Forever.

DETECTIVE MACDONALD: Explain yourself.

(shuffling around)

DETECTIVE MACDONALD: Geez . . . . Jesus. What is that?

ADAM: I told you. I'm marked by it.

DETECTIVE MACDONALD: Where . . . where did that come from?

ADAM: I told you. That other side. The Rainbow Filth . . . it's true what Hauser said—it's actually a portal to another dimension.

DETECTIVE MACDONALD: My God . . . . that marking, it's . . . does it cover your whole arm?

(more shuffling)

DETECTIVE MACDONALD: That's . . . . not possible.

ADAM: You can see it.

DETECTIVE MACDONALD: I think you need a doctor.

ADAM: No doctor will help me.

DETECTIVE MACDONALD: That's . . . . that looks really awful, kid.

ADAM: Want to hear how it happened?

DETECTIVE MACDONALD: I . . . I . . . of course, yes.

ADAM: It happened on the other side of the door. It happened to all of us . . . but . . . I'm pretty sure I was the only one to make it out alive.

Stepping through to the other side was like stepping through a waterfall—a cold wash froze my every nerve, and for three seconds my sensory system failed to process all the incoming sensations. It was like hugging a plugged-in toaster while bathing in ice water. Even after it was over, the crossing, it was like I would never be warm again. The six of us journeyed a few steps away from the access point, getting far enough away to where we felt safe from its power. I didn't think we'd ever be safe from it, but ten feet apart helped ease the trepidation.

I looked to Liz and she continued to ignore my presence, acting like I didn't exist. I wanted to talk to her, speak privately, but that wasn't in the cards.

After the thought of pulling her aside receded, I glanced at our surroundings. It was like we'd stumbled into a fairytale forest. Huge trees—with trunks as wide as cars—stood tall, far above your average California redwood. Lush leaves were in abundance, resting on the edge of far-protruding branches. The path was narrowed with excess foliage, but it wasn't slim enough to force us in another direction.

Everything was covered in the rainbow effect. It moved through all things. One of the auroras floated before me and I reached out, trying to touch it. It darted away like a fish terrified of experiencing human flesh—which I thought was a good sign. It meant the ribbon-like entities were not naturally predatory.

Hauser looked back at us with a smile and said, "Let's go. Let's see how far we can get."

I didn't like his smile or his words, but then again, there was nothing he could have said to make me like him more.

We journeyed up the muddy path, the soil below also taking on a rainbow-like quality, though more muted and dirtier.

We passed plants and flowers that were oddly colored, bright vegetation imbued with swirls of orange and red and blue and purple and yellow, the brightest versions of the primary colors. Prismatic floral arrangements. It was beautiful and I would have admired the place much more if I could have shaken the sense that, ultimately, this unexplored dimension was in some way harmful to us.

We pressed on, following Hauser's lead.

Twenty minutes later, I couldn't take it anymore. I came on this trip without any knowledge of what we were looking for, and now that I was here, saw this place existed with my own eyes—I needed to know what the fuck this whole thing was all about.

"Hauser," I said, jogging to catch up to him. "Hauser?"

The bastard ignored me.

"Hey," I said, grabbing his arm.

He spun on me and shoved me to the back of the line. "Get your hands off me," he snapped, and there was a primordial fire in his eyes, one I'd never seen before. In my brief interactions with the man, I always got the sense he was secretly a pacifist, but now . . . now I knew he wasn't. Whether the environment had something to do with the newly emerging and aggressive behavior, I didn't know.

"Hey, asshole," I responded, leaning forward and shoving him back. "What are we doing here?"

He sneered. "What are we doing here? What are we doing here? *We're here to discover the truth.*" The last sentence he spat through his teeth.

"The truth of what?" I couldn't help it—I laughed in his face. Then I turned, sweeping my vision across the others who'd taken the opportunity to use the confrontation as a break from walking. "I mean, do any of you know what this is about?"

Hauser bit his lip. "I knew bringing you along was going to fuck us up. But it had to be done."

"It had to be done? What does that mean?"

Liz started crying. "I'm so sorry!" she shouted. "I warned you. Warned you not to come."

Everyone was staring at me now, and I kinda hated it. I got the sense I should backtrack toward the door (and hastily), but the thought of leaving to go back alone made me queasy.

"What the fuck is going on?" I asked no one in particular. I would have accepted an answer from anyone, so long as it wasn't another mindfuck. "Tell me. The truth."

"I broke up with you," Liz said, crying into her hands now. "So you *wouldn't* be a part of this."

"Well, he is a part of this now," Hauser said, almost delightedly. "We have to do what we have to do, and we have to do it quickly."

"I'm not moving another inch until you tell me what the hell this place is and what is happening." I stood my ground and jammed a finger in Hauser's face. "Is this . . . is this even real?"

"It's real," Billy said, grabbing hold of some fruit I'd never seen before. It looked like a cross between a banana and a pear. Of course, it was multi-colored, yellow and green stripes running throughout it. "This fruit is real, and if I eat it, I will die."

"We can't disturb anything here," Hauser explained. "They do not like when we disturb their terrain."

"Who the fuck is 'they?' " I asked, expecting a response, but everyone shut their mouths and looked elsewhere. "I'm serious."

"You shouldn't have come," Liz said, gaining control of her emotions. She was still crying but had dammed the flow some. "Why did you come?"

"To help you." I laughed because it was obvious. At least, I thought it was. "To save you."

"There's no saving me, Adam. I thought you knew that. I thought you were smarter than that." She shrugged. "This is the life I've chosen."

"What the fuck are you talking about? This isn't . . . this isn't a life."

"But it is," Hauser said, and then clapped me on the shoulder. "You'll see soon enough—once you cross the plane, there is truly no coming back. Not in the traditional sense."

Hauser was right about that—I'd know soon enough.

*

After a short break, we traveled the path for another half hour or so. I kept my cool and didn't start any shit. Though . . . I really wanted to. I also couldn't ignore the way the twins were glaring at me, looking over their shoulders like they were planning to jump me at some point. Maybe they *were* planning that. I don't know. It could have been my paranoia creeping in. Ever since "crossing over," my entire sensory system felt rearranged and erratic. Maybe they weren't eyeing me up at all. But then again, maybe if things didn't go down the way they did over the next fifteen minutes, maybe they would have jumped me.

We arrived at a structure about five minutes after their eyes last left me. A temple made of stone and clay-colored brick stood like the end boss's lair in some old-school Nintendo game. It was a magnificent sight to see in this strange new world and the most normal thing we'd discovered so far. Massive columns held up the dentil-adorned pediment, giving it a very Roman temple vibe. What it was doing out here in the middle of the exotic forest, I had no idea, and since no one was volunteering any information, I assumed I'd never know. But it was out of place, that was for sure. Vines hung from the colorful trees, draping around the architectural beauty and strangling the stone columns. The loose foliage that drooped from the temple's contoured edges swayed in a noiseless wind. At the top of the long stairs (at least fifty steps to the landing), a black door rested in the center of the shape—a rectangular void that offered no assurance that this was a safe haven, a break from what could have been a very inhospitable environment.

Hauser marched up the stairs, ignoring the floating rainbow amoebas that passed before him. I still wanted to touch one, but the second I reached out, Liz grabbed my hand and forcefully tore it down. It was the first time she'd touched me in . . . I dunno. Weeks? A month? Since before she left for Cambodia?

It had been a long time since our skin met. Even though the conditions of this interaction weren't exactly amicable, it still felt cozy to me.

"Liz . . ." I said, reaching out for her hand, thinking she might entertain the thought now that we were here, together, in the middle of this absolute weirdness.

"Don't," she said, "touch anything. You don't want that shit on you."

I didn't know what she meant at the time, but I guess I do now. You've seen their effect firsthand, Detective. But don't tell me you wouldn't have tried to touch them. You would have. The floaty amoeba things that flickered with that prismatic, translucent glimmer were something that would latch onto you if touched. Much like a leech itself. Sometimes I chuckle about that, the irony of the events, how they unfolded.

But sometimes I cry, too.

"Come on," Hauser said from the top step. "We mustn't delay."

Billy and Deana got to the top in a few steps, the twins following closely behind. Liz and I brought up the rear. Everyone dipped inside the black door hastily, but I wasn't as fast to surrender my body to that darkness. Not yet. I had a real issue with walking into that space, even though the others had gone through so easily.

"Come on," Liz said, sensing my horror. "It will be okay."

"Will it?"

Her eyes told me it would not be.

"Why do I get the sense there's no coming back once I cross that doorway?" A drifting shimmer passed before my eyes, and I leaned back to avoid contact. "Huh?"

"We've already accessed the point of no return," she said. "Whatever happens next does not matter."

"You're speaking to me in riddles, Liz. Just tell me—what's beyond that door?"

Her eyes sparkled with life for the first time since she came home. It was like whatever mystery awaiting us on the other side was treasure for the soul. The gift of eternal bliss. But I couldn't get on board with that theory.

Nothing good was waiting for us. I knew that. I had always known that.

"You'll have to witness it with your own eyes," she said, and passed on through to the other side.

Of course I followed, immersing myself in the all-black portal that felt very cold and sticky and impossibly sinister.

Recording

Property of the Shrewsbury Police

Saturday/June 2nd, 2024/9:28 p.m.
Interviewing Detective: Chase MacDonald
Witness/Suspect: Adam Godfrey

DETECTIVE MACDONALD: Jesus Christ, kid. You're telling me—

ADAM: I'm telling you what happened. That's all I can tell. I'll take a polygraph if you don't believe me.

DETECTIVE MACDONALD: Yeah, lotta good that will do. You're so crazy that you probably believe this bullshit, would probably pass the poly with flying colors.

ADAM: It did happen. All of what I've told you. And what I'm about to tell you.

DETECTIVE MACDONALD: You mean, what was in that temple . . .

ADAM: Exactly. I really hope you keep an open mind through all of this. Because even though everything I've told you so far is the truth, I realize how the following will sound to the untrained ear.

DETECTIVE MACDONALD: Untrained?

ADAM: You haven't witnessed what else is out there, beyond reality.

DETECTIVE MACDONALD: Rainbow worlds?

ADAM: Other worlds too, not just that one. Our minds are limited to just this one world, the reality that has been built up all around us. Certain additives to our chemical makeup can change that, alter your perception of reality and take you to these other dimensions. You see, the worlds exist *inside* us.

DETECTIVE MACDONALD: Worlds exist inside us. *(humorless laugh)* You sure are a crackpot, ain't you, Godfrey?

ADAM: I'm sure that's what they'll say. I'm sure that's the easiest explanation. But I'm just enlightened, man. I've seen what happens when reality's veil is lowered and what awaits us on the other side.

DETECTIVE MACDONALD: Okay. Sure, sure. Let's just have it out with your story. Finish it up.

ADAM: Okay. Just want to warn you—this next part is . . . well, it's wild.

DETECTIVE MACDONALD: I'm sure it can't be any more unbelievable than what you've already told me.

ADAM: Heh . . . I wish.

At first there was nothingness, and the nothingness lasted for a solid minute. The cold, liquid rush that encompassed my entire body and seeped into every pore froze me, every part of me. I couldn't move, couldn't speak—I felt like Han Solo in the Carbonite fridge. Just . . . *stuck*. But alive.

A minute later and I was free. Released, I was able to get my feet moving. At first it was like walking against a strong gust of wind. My shoe bottoms were sticking to the ground, like shuffling across a movie theater aisle after a stupid kids' movie let out. But soon after, the motion of the world returned to a somewhat normal balance of gravity and earthly mechanics, and the world no longer felt viscous. Then the darkness faded, and dim natural light appeared, just enough to see where I was going. I saw shadows before me, human shapes, then realized it was my companions all moving toward the same destination inside the temple. When things became clearer, the dark hallway opened to a torchlit chamber with just enough flickering luminance to see the far wall. Before I noticed the monstrosity across from us, I took a few seconds to soak in the calmness, a break from the abstract world I'd just stepped away from. There were no prismatic reflections or rainbow trees, a colorful curtain that had been pulled over the world. The temple was absent from these otherworldly peculiarities, and we were saved from the weirdness of this distant reality, at least for the moment. For the second.

For the instant.

My eyes were drawn to the ceiling, and I noticed some vegetation that had snaked its way through the cracks in the stone formation, worming through the spaces to spread across the corners and run down the walls. Serpentine coils of purple vines had crept out of these faults and all of them—twenty extensions—met in the center of the far wall. Where the monstrosity waited.

Waited for us.

Before I describe this thing, I want you to picture a king's throne made of skulls—not exactly human; too oblong and misshapen, but close enough to qualify, I suppose. A pile of bones and decaying remains at its base, just sitting there on display for all to see, a tactic that one could interpret as a warning to all who enter. Okay, this *thing* sitting on the throne had me guessing what it was for a solid beat. It was human-shaped, though anatomically speaking, it was all off. One arm was longer than the other, the left stunted as if it had been cut off at the elbow and grew back just the hand. One leg was completely missing— at least I thought it was. Upon closer inspection, the unclothed form of this man (let's call it that) had sunken into the royal throne, as if the man's body was once liquid— or maybe the seat itself was—and one of the components had been absorbed by the other and then solidified halfway through the amalgamation process. In the backrest, a face was centered, forehead exposed, the back half of its head submerged into the iron chair. Its eyes, white orbs that held no pupils, blinked, letting us know that the being was alive. Purple lips opened and closed, reminding me of a dry fish.

Hauser crept closer to the throne as if he was approaching an injured animal, fearful of being lashed out at. He even stuck out his hand, testing the distance between them, which only amounted to about ten feet. "Walter," he said, and my heart skipped.

Walter? Walter Bogie?

"Walter, it's me," he said. "We've come back. We . . . we've all been really sick, but we've . . . we've brought someone else. Someone who can make things right with *them*."

Sweat began to pour from me. My shirt was soaked around the collar, under the arms. I took a step back and bumped into the twins.

They didn't move, didn't step aside to let me pass.

"See?" Hauser said, pointing at me. If Walter had pupils, they might have gazed upon me.

"Outsider . . . " the Walter-Thing said. *"The Rainbow*

collects. The Rainbow collects . . . outsiders?" He said this as if asking a question.

Hauser seemed to speak the language perfectly. "Yes, yes. I know. We're here to give them what they want."

Now I wanted to run. Needed to, really—I had no other option. I turned to sprint back toward the portal, but before I could take a step, the Hurt twins hooked their arms under mine, so I couldn't go anywhere. Their calculated move locked my arms, so I couldn't throw a punch. I kicked at their shins, but it did nothing to help release me.

"Fuck off me!" I shouted.

They only laughed at my struggle.

"It's okay," Billy said, his voice somber. I could tell he wasn't completely on board with whatever was going down, but also—it was like he had no choice. It was this or some alternative disaster. "We didn't want this, but you persisted."

"You had to butt in," Deana added.

"You could have left it alone," offered one of the twins, and I couldn't tell which one because I was too busy trying to wrench myself free. "But you just had to press us about Hauser, about this place. About our adventures."

"You said no one else went in!" I shouted at Billy, surprised that this was the first thing on my mind at the moment.

"I lied, okay?" Billy threw his hands up in a beyond frustrated sort of way, like he was the one currently being held against his will. Fuck Billy. I promised myself if I broke free, he was the first one I was going after. Mostly because I considered him a friend, the only one in the group other than Liz I could trust. He'd betrayed me worst of all. "I fucking lied. Look, man. It's fine. We have to do this one thing, and it all ends. Just a tiny little thing, okay?"

"What thing?" I asked, trembling with rage. "What the fuck do you want with me?"

Liz avoided my probing stare. Billy also looked away,

but he returned a few seconds later when it was obvious no one else would clue me in.

"This place . . . the creatures that live here at . . . at the end of the rainbow . . . they require a sacrifice in exchange for passage to the next plane. There's a trade and—"

"You're not sacrificing me to some creatures!" I screamed as I bucked in the twins' arms. I thrashed and kicked, but none of it helped. In fact, one of the twins—Arthur, I think—bashed my nose in with the heel of his right palm. I heard the bone crack and felt blood leaking down my upper lip almost immediately. The nose was broken for sure, but that didn't stop me from trying to squirm free. "You're not feeding me to some—"

"Whoa!" Billy said, holding up his hands, asking everyone to chill, not just me. "Relax. No one said anything about feeding anyone to anything."

I glanced at the human shape on the throne, the languid movements of its malformed limbs. If that was my impending fate, then I would have preferred a swift execution right then and there.

Hauser finally faced me, taking charge of the situation and abandoning the conversation with his old friend, assuming the story he'd previously told me was true. I assumed he'd lied about the whole suicide thing. Or maybe he hadn't. Maybe Walter had taken his own life by resigning himself to this alternate reality. In a way, I guess if he chose to remain here in this state, it was the same as putting a gun under his chin and pulling the trigger.

"Godfrey," Hauser said calmly. "I need you to shut up, listen, and trust us. You are a vital part of this process, and you're not going to fuck it up."

"Am I in danger?"

He didn't answer right away, so I knew I was. "No," he said, without the confidence I was expecting, *needing* to carry on. "I don't think so. There's something that has to happen, something unpleasant, but not exactly harmful to you. There's something this place requires from you."

"What's that?" I continued to focus on Walter's stunted arm, the weird hand that had grown back, the fingers curled like dry, twisted noodles. "What does it want from me?"

He noticed me gawking at Walter because the next words out of his mouth were, "Don't worry about Walter. He's not important. What happened to him won't happen to us. As long as you play by the rules."

"Rules?" I scoffed. "This doesn't seem like a place with many rules."

His dim expression darkened. "All places have rules, Godfrey. A world without rules would be chaos. This is a beautiful world, not some chaotic realm unbound. Now, Godfrey. Please listen to me. In about fifteen seconds, they are going to come for you."

"They?"

He swallowed. "We have no name for them."

At this, the old man who'd become one with the throne let go of a throaty chuckle. *"No name,"* he husked. *"No name for them."*

This terrified me, caused a rush of panic to ascend my stomach and infiltrate my chest, but I still couldn't break for the exit. The twins' grasp on me had only strengthened as time passed. That, or I had become so afraid that I couldn't feel my muscles.

"What . . . I don't understand."

But I would soon enough. There was movement beneath my feet, a rattle like nearby thunder. Scratching sounds, nails against the other side of the clay-brick walls. An awkward moaning sound; like, in the right context, the noise could have been confused for someone experiencing a moment of sexual ecstasy. More than one voice, which put me more on edge.

Hauser's expression softened. He put a finger to his lips, demanding my silence. In the grim atmosphere, the chalky-stale smell of this ancient temple was suddenly replaced by something foul and overpowering, like an untreated wound gone violently putrid.

And then I saw them. From the shadows in the opposite corner of the room, three bodies appeared. Humanoid figures with poor spinal curvatures, so badly arched forward that their chests were near their knees as they crouch-walked out. They were hairless beings, their skin smooth with diamond-like scales, which changed color with each movement, a dirty-rainbow palette. Dark green fluids thick as steak sauce dripped from their open mouths, and the moaning continued with each step, a low, guttural vocalization that was utterly primal, a noise that matched their appearance. As they got closer, I could make out the details of their features, their demonic, orc-like qualities. Piglike noses that seemed to have been smashed in on themselves. Ears that tapered to a pitchfork's point. Deep pockmarks on the flesh around the eyes that looked like asteroid craters. Misshapen skulls with no definable pattern sporting tumorous knobs that sat like air bubbles rising to the surface of a dark lake.

I noticed the skulls around Walter's feet had belonged to these creatures, whatever they were. Perhaps they were indigenous to this dimension, or maybe they were like us— accidental wanderers found in an unfortunate situation. Or not. Maybe they were the rulers of this parasitic realm.

"The fuck . . . " I said, the rest of what I wanted to say lost in my struggle for oxygen.

"Relax," Hauser instructed. "Don't speak. Let them take what they want. Let them move on. It will only take a minute."

A minute? A minute in the wrong circumstances could easily feel like hours.

At first they sniffed me, like I was some desirable meal they wished to sample. Their noses inches from my neck, I involuntarily constricted. The twins kept me where I was, still as they could. Unafraid of these hairless bipeds, they stood like guardians, though I sensed if the trio wished to drag me off and have their way with me, the Hurt twins wouldn't hesitate to surrender my flesh.

I felt the creatures' collective breath on my neck. I closed my eyes, unable to look at what was about to become of me. I imagined one of them clamping their teeth around my throat and severing my jugular. That didn't happen, of course, and when I opened my eyes, one of them was peering directly up at me. I gazed into those white orbs for eyes and begged with my own; for mercy, for permission to live past this moment.

My wish was granted, but Hauser had not been wrong about the sacrifice—one needed to occur, and I had no clue what the things wanted from me, so I continued to stare back at them innocently, pleading silently, hoping they could see me through the milky haze that covered their oblong eyes.

One of them licked me. I felt the slime of its tongue slip up my cheek, leaving a trail of tacky jelly in its wake. The practiced movement unnerved me to my core. Visibly shaking now, I wished for this sequence to end, hoping I would survive the conclusion, whatever came next. Then, I felt the slimy slug of a tongue enter my ear canal. The muscle had a rough texture, almost like a cat's, the sandpapery feeling beginning to push past the boundaries of my anatomy. It was like the tongue folded on itself as it moved forward, squirming toward the inside of my head, forming a cone shape to drill into the center of me. I couldn't believe it, but also—I couldn't fight it.

Then, my other ear became wet with the same sensation. One on each end, sticking their alien tongues inside my head, licking, tasting, sampling whatever it was they'd come to take from me.

The third being continued to look up at me. Then it opened its mouth, spilling streams of dark, greenish saliva. A tongue came forth like a timid night critter poking its head out of the trash. One of the twins held my head by my hair, making sure I didn't attempt to wiggle or avoid the next portion of this examination. The other twin lowered my jaw for me—I didn't fight. I was paralyzed. By fear mostly, but also, something else. An empty feeling overtook me, and I lacked the energy to combat the attack if that's what this was.

The tongue entered my mouth, my throat. The taste was so overwhelmingly sour and sickening that I wanted to vomit. My stomach tried to reject this ceremony, but nothing came up. Even though the tongue pushed farther inside me, I did not choke. I could breathe just fine, and I didn't know how, other than my nostrils were still pulling in and letting go of clean, breathable air.

My eyes rolled back. I felt a wave of sleep crash over me, pulling me under the tides of unconsciousness.

Hauser walked over to me, smiled, and said, "It's almost over."

And then it was.

I woke up sometime later, disoriented. My surroundings were unclear, but as the light began to focus and the pieces of scenery matured into definable shapes, I understood I was still inside the temple. A rainbow haze had entered the room, projecting prismatic reflections on us, the walls, and of course, Walter Bogie.

"What . . . " I asked, but my throat was too sore for words to pass through it. My entire esophagus felt bruised, like someone had throat-punched me. A dry swallow brought pain.

Hauser was kneeling before me, hands clasped on his knee, that fucking smile resting on his face. Like he was proud of me or something. "You did well," he said, touching my knee with a certain affection that filled me with more disgust. "The transaction was complete. We will all ascend to the next plane. We will get to meet *them*."

"I thought . . . " I coughed, still having a hard time getting the words out, but I needed to. I fought through the burn that raged in my throat. "I thought . . . *they* were *them*." I nodded to the space in the temple where those hairless creatures had formed. They were gone now, no evidence that they'd ever existed in the first place.

"Hardly. Guardians of this realm, perhaps. Not sure. They strip something from you, from your mind, granting you access to that next level."

"What . . ."

"You don't feel it?"

I didn't feel anything save for that violent headache and sore throat.

"You don't feel less?" he asked, arching his eyebrows. "But also . . . so much more?"

I shook my head.

"You will," he said, patting my knee again, like a good boy. Then he stood up. Went over to the wall where the Sunken Man sat on his throne, still and dead-like. "Walter. We are ready to discover the next plane."

The others stood behind their professor, each of them eager to reach that next level. I glanced back at the door and the tunnel we'd taken to get here. I had my strength back, could move my legs just fine. Running out of here was an option.

But would they let me leave?

I got the sense that I was stuck here, even if they didn't stop me. I didn't know the way back through the Rainbow Forest and getting lost in this alternate reality was not something I desired.

But talking to Liz was. Saving her. Bringing her back alive. Bringing her back to normal.

But in that moment I saw the look in her eye. The determination. The desire to continue, witness the secrets beyond this current reality. What awaited them all beyond the gates of this next level.

There was no bringing her back, I decided. She was lost, gone to the Rainbow Filth that infected her brain.

I had to try one last time, though. One last attempt to bring her back.

"Liz," I said, sneaking up behind her. My voice sounded like a sick frog. "Can we . . . talk?"

She finally turned my way. In the background, Hauser was pleading with Walter to grant them access to the next level, and the Sunken Man was beginning to reanimate.

"What?" she asked as if my question infuriated her to some degree.

"Can we . . . talk?"

"About?"

"Us?"

Her eyelids fluttered. "There is no us."

"How can you say that? After three years, how can you just throw us away like that?"

She didn't respond. Not at first. I thought she was going to turn her back on me, but after a twenty-second delay, she came back with, "We don't live in a fairytale. This doesn't have a happy ending."

"I'm not asking for a fairytale. I'm asking . . . for you . . . to be with me."

"It's over, Adam." She went to turn, but I gripped her shoulder. "Adam, stop—"

"Will you marry me?" I dropped one knee to the hard surface.

"What?"

I hadn't planned this out, didn't have a fucking clue what I was doing, but . . . it felt right to propose to her. Here. In this moment. Before the others. She needed to know I was committed to her, now and forever. Whether she accepted it or not didn't matter. What mattered was that she knew.

"Will. You. Marry. Me." I could feel Hauser's hard glare on me, and I reveled in that knowledge. No matter what answer I would receive, it was those seconds I would cherish for a long, long time.

"No, Adam. I will not." And then she took her hands back and spun away from me.

I would never make eye contact with her again.

"Bummer, dude," said one of the twins. The other chuckled.

I expected Hauser to flash me that patented evil smile of his, but instead, he nodded, out of what I perceived to be some mutual respect.

It was the last time I would make eye contact with him.

That was a minute before everything came undone and the portal to the next plane opened up.

The rainbow glow intensified, a smoky fog billowing into the room, materializing from nothing. Visibility soon became so unclear that I could no longer make out the walls of the room. I can't really explain it other than the temple suddenly felt much bigger, as if the walls themselves had collapsed and we were suddenly outside, back in the field where this whole thing started. Everything felt open, limitless, and continuously stretching. My perception of what I thought I understood of this place suddenly felt very wrong.

"It's here," Hauser said from somewhere up ahead, though I couldn't see him. The rainbow mist guarded all things in front me. Even Liz. Even my own hands. "It's the next plane, I can see—"

A cracking sound that reminded me of a whip hitting hide interrupted the man's announcement. There was a short choking sound and a sharp clicking, like the relief of pressure between two joints. There was silence after that, until someone—I think it was Billy—said, "Professor Hauser?"

That's when something hard hit me in the chest. Like a football being hurled at me from close range by a professional quarterback. Instinctively, my arms reacted to the projectile and I caught the object, trapping it against my chest. It was sticky with wetness, and when I looked down after using one arm to clear away the rainbow smoke so I *could* see, I saw Lewis Hauser's lifeless eyes staring up me. His head had been wrenched free from the shoulders, the flesh of his neck torn to rags, the cervical vertebrae that stuck out mangled and snapped most uncleanly, the jagged bone looking like broken, chipped teeth in a mouth full of blood. There was red all over me, which looked too dark to be blood in the rainbow exhibit.

I dropped the severed head on the floor. It vanished into the mist below and landed with a wet smack. Backing away from whatever had done this, I listened to the screams of the others. Shadows whipped through the hazy atmosphere, and it took me about three seconds to realize that the dark shapes were more of Hauser, his limbs sailing through the air. His torso zoomed past me, splashing more of his blood against me as it went shooting past. Shadows shaped like thick tree branches whipped in the near distance. Screams were severed as the arms of this great beast—eight in total—combed the immediate area for more targets.

I didn't hesitate now. I turned and sprinted in the opposite direction, running full speed, not caring if there was something in the rainbow waiting for me to make my escape. I darted through the fog, ignoring the whipping sounds, the air being displaced at high volumes. Ran where my directional sense told me the exit was, that black door that led us into the temple. About twenty meters later, I slipped in what I thought was mud, but after looking down I noticed my foot was snagged on a mushy, decaying carcass—only it wasn't human. It was one of those hairless creatures, the one that made tongue-love to my ear canals. Its body was splayed open, revealing its peculiar bone structure and oddly-shaped anatomy. Its black blood slicked my right pant leg.

I scrambled on.

Toward the door.

Toward home.

Somehow—I don't know how—I reached it.

I was released from The Rainbow Filth.

When I got back to the field, Annabelle Gump was gone. The fire she'd lit had been extinguished. No note, no nothing.

No sign that she had ever been there.

Recording
Property of the Shrewsbury Police

Saturday/June 2nd, 2024/10:35 p.m.
Interviewing Detective: Chase MacDonald
Witness/Suspect: Adam Godfrey

DETECTIVE MACDONALD: Okaaaaay then.

ADAM: Told you to keep an open mind.

DETECTIVE MACDONALD: Kid, there's no way you could possibly think I'd believe that.

ADAM: No, I suppose you wouldn't. If someone had told me that story, I'd think that person is a bonafide maniac too.

DETECTIVE MACDONALD: I'm glad you can see that.

ADAM: So, where's the fitting?

DETECTIVE MACDONALD: Fitting? I don't follow.

ADAM: For the straitjacket.

DETECTIVE MACDONALD: Good to see you still have a sense of humor after this. Especially since you just said you witnessed the murder of Lewis Hauser, your girlfriend, and four other individuals.

ADAM: I only saw Lew, remember? I don't know what happened to the others. Liz . . . she could still be out there, I guess, where the Rainbow ends.

DETECTIVE MACDONALD: Right. And the other blood sample on your clothing, the mystery blood—you trying to convince me it belongs to some . . . creature?

ADAM: Humanoid species, yes. Possibly indigenous to that plane.

DETECTIVE MACDONALD: Hmm. And what's going to happen when that comes back from the lab as human DNA?

ADAM: I'll eat my hat.

DETECTIVE MACDONALD: You're not wearing a hat.

ADAM: Exactly.

DETECTIVE MACDONALD: (sighing) Kid, I'mma let you stew for a few minutes. I need to piss something fierce and discuss some things with my colleagues. Can you sit tight for a bit?

ADAM: Is that a little cop humor? Hilarious. And you should really double-check that blood sample. The results from the lab should be back by now.

DETECTIVE MACDONALD: I'll do that.

(chair scraping floor, footsteps, door opening, closing)

(silence)

(incoherent whispering)

(incoherent whispering continues)

ADAM: *(whispering, unclear) here? (whispering, unclear) worthy? I will be (whispering, unclear). (whispering, unclear) plane. Help me, and I will (whispering, unclear). I just (whispering, unclear) back. Liz? Remember. (whispering, unclear)*

(twenty seconds of silence)

ADAM: *I understand. I will wait for the signal. I will (whispering, unclear)*

(laughing)

Detective Chase "Mac" MacDonald left room three, walked halfway down the hall, and then doubled back. He rubbed his throbbing temples and shut his eyes until the door, several feet from the interrogation room he'd occupied for the last four hours, opened. Carla Robinson strolled out into the hallway, her eyebrows arched.

"How'd it go in there?" she asked.

"You weren't watching?"

"Couldn't. Had a call."

"How convenient."

"What's the scoop?"

Mac ran a hand through his graying strands of hair. He'd let it grow a tad longer than the wife liked, but that was okay—he liked it, and that was all that mattered to him. Vivian would get used to it. "Well, the kid's crazier than two bags of cats. Told me some nonsense story that makes zero sense. Wild delusions. He all but admitted to getting hopped up on some crank and killing Hauser. Blamed it on some otherworldly creatures—fucking craziest thing I've ever heard, Car. You have to listen to the recording. It's good for a few laughs."

"Oh, I will."

"We have enough to hold him."

"Kid's lawyer is here."

Mac laughed. "Well, once they hear what's on that tape, they'll be begging for a deal."

"Insanity plea?"

"That'd be my guess. We should get a psych eval done ASAP."

"I'll put in for it," Carla told him, "though I'm sure the kid's legal team will want to have it done third-party."

"Oh hey—meant to ask," Mac said. "The DNA samples come back from the lab? Like, the final report?"

"Oh yeah, that's who I was on the phone with."

"And?"

"Hauser's confirmed. The other sample came back inconclusive."

"Inconclusive?" Something frigid leaked under his skin. "Well . . . what did they say?"

"It was weird—they couldn't confirm the blood was human. 'No other human DNA present' was the official statement."

"Seriously?" His skin felt clammy.

"Seriously."

"Was it . . . from some animal?"

"If it was, they would have said so. *Inconclusive* is the best they could come up with." She shrugged in an *Oh well, can't win them all* sort of way. "Doesn't mean anything. Just means the sample was too dirty or insufficient to—what? What is it? Why are you looking at me like that?"

He didn't answer at first, his thoughts suddenly getting lost in the intricate maze of what Godfrey had told him. Godfrey had wished him luck regarding the second sample. Because he knew it would come back inconclusive.

Because what he'd said was true. All of it.

Which was impossible, and Mac didn't believe it for a second. Couldn't.

"Hello? Mac?" Carla snapped her fingers in front of his eyes. "You still with me?"

"Yeah," he said hoarsely. "Yeah, sorry."

"You went spacey on me."

"Been a long afternoon."

"It's almost eleven."

"Exactly." He checked his watch. "I gotta call Viv. She's probably pissed as hell. Oh, and you'll want to get the kid to a doctor. Something is fucked up on his arm. Don't know what it is." He checked his phone. Three missed calls. "Shit—I gotta call her."

"Go for it. I'm meeting the lawyer in—ah, there she is."

Mac spun, following Carla's eyes. A woman holding a brown-leather briefcase strutted down the hallway, her stony face revealing no expression. Mac immediately thought two things—one, this woman was a robot, incapable of processing human emotion whatsoever, advantageous for a lawyer he supposed. And two, he knew this woman despite never meeting her. He couldn't place a finger on how this was, but he *did* know her.

Mac nodded at Carla and moved down the hall. He flashed the woman a quick, genial smile as he passed, but she did not acknowledge him. She passed him without bothering to make eye contact.

All business, Mac thought, and in most cases, it was better that way.

He moved toward the exit where he would have his cigarette and call Viv. Just before he reached the door, he heard the woman introduce herself to Carla.

"Annabelle Gump," she said discreetly. "I'm representing the Godfrey boy."

THANK YOU

So many people to thank, and sorry in advance if I left you out—it certainly wasn't intentional. First off, thanks to Max Booth III and Lori Michelle for taking on this weirdo novella. When I wrote it I was pretty sure no one would love it like I loved it, so to have a home for it at Ghoulish is something special, and I'm totally honored. Shout out to some of coolest writerly people I know, who've kept me sane and have motivated me, inspired me (for one reason or another) to keep on writing these last couple of years, especially when things were tough (in no particular order): Chad Lutzke, Frank Edler, JC Walsh, Kenneth W. Cain, Izzy Lee, Patrick Lacey, Hunter Shea, Ross Jeffery, Laurel Hightower, Sadie Hartmann, Andrew at DarkLit Press, Jonathan Janz, Ronald Malfi, Clay McLeod Chapman, and my film/television agent, Karmen Wells. Also, a huge shoutout to my wife, Ashley, my favorite non-reader, who's always there to support me, no matter what; I would totally follow you into the Rainbow Filth and back, forever.

ABOUT THE AUTHOR

Tim Meyer dwells in a dark cave near the Jersey Shore. He's the author of more than fifteen novels, including *Malignant Summer, The Switch House, Dead Daughters, Limbs,* and many other titles. When he's not working on the next book, he's usually hanging out with his wife and son, shooting around on the basketball court, playing video games, or messing with a new screenplay. He bleeds coffee and IPAs.

You can learn more about his books at timmeyerwrites.com.

SPOOKY TALES FROM GHOULISH BOOKS 2023

LIKE REAL | Shelly Lyons

ISBN: 978-1-943720-82-8 $16.95

This mind-bending body horror rom-com is a rollicking Cronenbergian gene splice of *Idle Hands* and *How to Lose a Guy in 10 Days*. It's freaky. It's fun. It's LIKE REAL.

XCRMNTMNTN | Andrew Hilbert

ISBN: 978-1-943720-81-1 $14.95

When a pile of shit from space lands near a renowned filmmaker's set, inspiration strikes. Take a journey up a cosmic mountain of excrement with the director and his film crew as they ascend into madness led only by their own vanity and obsession. This is a nightmare about creation. This is a dream about poop. This is a call to arms against vowels. This is *XCRMNTMNTN*.

BOUND IN FLESH | edited by Lor Gislason

ISBN: 978-1-943720-83-5 $16.95

Bound in Flesh: An Anthology of Trans Body Horror brings together 13 trans and non-binary writers, using horror to both explore the darkest depths of the genre and the boundaries of flesh. A disgusting good time for all! Featuring stories by Hailey Piper, Joe Koch, Bitter Karella, and others.

CONJURING THE WITCH | Jessica Leonard

ISBN: 978-1-943720-84-2 $16.95

Conjuring the Witch is a dark, haunted story about what those in power are willing to do to stay in power, and the sins we convince ourselves are forgivable.

WHAT HAPPENED WAS IMPOSSIBLE |
E. F. Schraeder

ISBN: 978-1-943720-85-9 $14.95

Everyone knows the woman who escapes a massacre is a final girl, but who is the final boy? *What Happened Was Impossible* follows the life of Ida Wright, a man who knows how to capitalize on his childhood tragedies . . . even when he caused them.

THE ONLY SAFE PLACE LEFT IS THE DARK|
Warren Wagner
ISBN: 978-1-943720-86-6 $14.95

In *The Only Safe Place Left is the Dark*, an HIV positive gay man must leave the relative safety of his cabin in the woods to brave the zombie apocalypse and find the medication he needs to stay alive.

THE SCREAMING CHILD| Scott Adlerberg
ISBN: 978-1-943720-87-3 $16.95

Scott Adlerberg's *The Screaming Child* is a mystery horror novel told by a grieving woman working on a book about an explorer who was murdered in a remote wilderness region, only to get caught up in a dangerous journey after hearing the distant screams from her own vanished child somewhere in the woods.

RAINBOW FILTH | Tim Meyer
ISBN: 978-1-943720-88-0 $14.95

Rainbow Filth is a weirdo horror novella about a small cult that believes a rare psychedelic substance can physically transport them to another universe.

LET THE WOODS KEEP OUR BODIES| E. M. Roy
ISBN: 978-1-943720-89-7 $16.95

The familiar becomes strange the longer you look at it. Leo Bates navigates a broken sense of reality, shattered memories, and a distrust of herself in order to find her girlfriend Tate and restore balance to their hometown of Eston—if such a thing ever existed to begin with.

SAINT GRIT| Kayli Scholz
ISBN: 978-1-943720-90-3 $14.95

One brooding summer, Nadine Boone pricks herself on a poisonous manchineel tree in the Florida backcountry. Upon self-orgasm, Nadine conjures a witch that she calls Saint Grit. Pitched as *Gummo* meets *The Craft*, Saint Grit grows inside of Nadine over three decades, wreaking repulsive havoc on a suspicious cast of characters in a small town known as Sugar Bends. Comes in Censored or Uncensored cover.

Ghoulish Books
PO Box 1104
Cibolo, TX 78108

☐ LIKE REAL   16.95
☐ XCRMNTMNTN   14.95
☐ BOUND IN FLESH   16.95
☐ CONJURING THE WITCH   16.95
☐ WHAT HAPPENED WAS IMPOSSIBLE   14.95
☐ THE ONLY SAFE PLACE LEFT IS THE DARK   14.95
☐ THE SCREAMING CHILD   16.95
☐ RAINBOW FILTH   14.95
☐ LET THE WOODS KEEP OUR BODIES   16.95
☐ SAINT GRIT   14.95
   Censored | Uncensored

Ship to:

Name   _____

Address _____

City_____State_____Zip _____

Phone Number _____

Book Total: $_____

Shipping Total: $_____

Grand Total: $_____

Not all titles available for immediate shipping. All credit card purchases must be made online at GhoulishBooks.com. Shipping is 5.80 for one book and an additional dollar for each additional book. Contact us for international shipping prices. All checks and money orders should be made payable to Perpetual Motion Machine.

Patreon:
www.patreon.com/pmmpublishing

Website:
www.GhoulishBooks.com

Facebook:
www.facebook.com/GhoulishBooks

Twitter:
@GhoulishBooks

Instagram:
@GhoulishBookstore

Newsletter:
www.PMMPNews.com

Linktree:
linktr.ee/ghoulishbooks